Dr Sharon Blackie is an award-w
recognised teacher whose work
mythology and ecology. Her fi
Rooted, became a word-of-mouth ecofeminist bestseller across the UK and North America. Her second, *The Enchanted Life*, offered insights into the art of belonging, and the everyday magic that comes from deepening our connection to the natural world. Her work has been translated into multiple languages. *Foxfire, Wolfskin and Other Stories of Shapeshifting Women* is her first collection of short stories. Sharon lives on a smallholding in the Cambrian mountains of Mid Wales with her husband and dogs.

www.sharonblackie.net

Praise for *Foxfire, Wolfskin*:

'Sharon Blackie has wrought a new-old magic for our times: glorious, beautiful, passionate myths. They show who we could have been, and they give us a glimpse of a world-that-could-be.' Manda Scott, author of *A Treachery of Spies* and *Boudica*

'Part rally cry, part warning, part manifesto and all parts enchanting, Sharon Blackie's *Foxfire, Wolfskin* is a deeply evocative and haunting collection. I want to press this powerful book into the hands of everyone I know and say listen.' Holly Ringland, author of *The Lost Flowers of Alice Hart*

'A book for all the wild women ... *Foxfire, Wolfskin* is simply the most perfect thing. I love each and every placement of each word. A shapeshifting symphony, filled with love, longing, rage and desire. Love the wildness, the shapeshifting, the fearsomeness of it.' Jackie Morris, co-author of *The Lost Words* and *The Lost Spells*

'These stories are so beautifully written that there were sections which gave me actual goosebumps.' Emma R

'This is great storytelling – imaginative, engaging, often beautiful. More to the point, it's inspiring – telling of women who find their voice, their courage, their power, women who draw on nature and the environment to avenge, to rise again.' The Literary Shed

'If you enjoy the darker side of fairy tales and want to be stunned by the magical side of history, you will love this book!' Books Beyond the Story

'Sometimes I come across a book where the language is so beautiful and clever that I am in literary ecstasy; this is one of those books … These stories sing with a deep and passionate love for desolate and secluded countrysides, and are all about the power of women.' Emma's Book Blog

'This is a book to have on the bookshelf and enjoy in moments of need, it will make you dream and think, the perfect company in a solitary night.' Varietats

'Here is magic, heartbreak, love, fear and power. It is beautifully written and will make you laugh and cry.' Orlando Books

'Witchy, wild and wonderful.' Rachel Read It

FOXFIRE, WOLFSKIN

and other stories of

SHAPESHIFTING WOMEN

SHARON BLACKIE

Illustrated by Helen Nicholson

5 7 9 10 8 6 4

This paperback edition published in 2020 by September Publishing
First published in 2019 by September Publishing

Typeset by Ed Pickford

Printed in Denmark on paper from responsibly managed, sustainable sources by Nørhaven

ISBN 978-1-912836-24-6

September Publishing
www.septemberpublishing.org

Author's note

Most of the stories in this book are either reimaginings of older tales, or contain characters, beings and motifs which appear in older tales. To fully appreciate these new stories, then, or to understand who these characters are who are speaking, it may be helpful to know something about the older versions – not all of which are particularly well known outside their place of origin. And so, at the back of this book, you'll find a set of notes which indicate the inspirations for each of the stories, and brief outlines of the originals.

Contents

WOLFSKIN

SAY YOU GO alone into the woods. It's winter, and you're hungry. So you take up your rifle, put on your deerskin jacket and your boots lined with rabbit fur. Off you trot.

Say it's dawn, and the light in the woods is thin. Air clear, and snow on the ground to give the game away. Crow calling your name; ready-to-roost owl hooting its warning into fire-filled sky. Fledgling morning, Orion no more than a glimmer now, Hunter hanging over hunter.

But say you don't think much of all that. You're there to kill your dinner, not to admire the scenery.

Say you're tired; you were up late the night before. Slim pickings in the woods, and on you walk. Say you're tired as evening falls; the rabbit is still warm. A long way back home, and the mill house which takes you by surprise invites you in. So you go inside to spend the night. Tomorrow there might be hind. Make a fire in the parlour, skin and cook the rabbit. You climb into the loft to sleep. Leave the fire burning in the grate; hot air rises. Leave broth and bones in the pan for breakfast.

Say you hear the door open just as you're falling asleep. Door creaks, like all the best stories say. Say a wolf comes in.

Sniffs; smells something tasty. Say she goes to the fire; raises herself up on her hind legs, shouts, *Skin down! Skin down!* Sure enough, down comes her skin. Slips out of it, and out slips a woman. The mill house is her home. Hangs the skin up on a peg behind the door, goes back to the fire, gnaws bones, drinks warm broth, falls asleep on the rush mat.

Say you watch this from a hole in the loft's wooden floor. Say you creep down the ladder and snatch away the wolf-woman's skin. Nail it to the mill wheel, tight and true. Walk over to the fire and nudge the wolf-woman with your foot. Say she screams, *Skin on me! Skin on me!* but it's the mill wheel the skin is on.

The wolf-woman cries.

Say you laugh.

Ha ha ha.

You know the rest. Wolf-woman has to marry man, because man has her skin. Man moves into enchanted mill; wolf-woman cleans and cooks. Same old story. Say you tell her you like stories; make her tell you stories each night before bed. Wolf-stories; they make you laugh. Promise to give her skin back if she tells you a story you really like.

But say you actually decide to sell the skin; it'll fetch a pretty price. Didn't even have to skin the wolf; it came ready made for sale. Say the wolf-woman sees that her skin is gone, and cries.

Say you laugh.

Ha ha ha.

Say the wolf-woman begins pregnant with hope, but ends up pregnant with a man-child. Say the man-child kills his brother Hope in the womb.

Don't you like this story? Say you do. You don't seem to be laughing now.

Well then: say the man-child hears people whisper that his mother is really a wolf. *Mama!* he says. *Are you a wolf?*

What nonsense, says the mother, and turns away.

Say the man-child asks his father whether his mother is a wolf. Father says yes. Man-child asks father where his mother's skin is. Father says he sold it.

Say the man-child starts to wonder whether he is a wolf too. Asks his mother how to find his wolf-skin. Say she tells him only his mother can show him how to discover his skin, and only when she's a wolf. The boy cries.

Say you laugh for the third time.

Ha ha ha.

Say the father sends the man-child over to the preacher's house. Takes a fresh buckskin and a basket of buns. Man-child smells his mother there, but mother is at home. Man-child sniffs; follows his nose. Follows his wolf-nose to the wolf-skin thrown on the seat of the preacher-man's wooden bench. Say he goes home and says to his mother, *Mama, Mama! I know where your skin is!*

Say the wolf-woman has lost her skin, but still has a wolf's bones. Say the wolf-woman has lost her skin, but still has a wolf's heart. Say the wolf-woman has lost her skin, but still has a wolf's eyes. Say the wolf-woman creeps out in the dark while her husband is away hunting, and steals through the window of the preacher's house. *Skin on me!* she says. And on the skin comes. Skin reaches for her, clamps around her, tightens. Caresses her like a lover, and she shudders. Skin flows all over her, down her back, around her thighs. Skin wraps itself softly around her throat, loosens her hurt heart.

Say the hunter comes home to find his wife gone and a wolf sitting in the kitchen. The cub is alongside. Say the wolf growls and bares its teeth. Say you never see it coming.

Say the wolf gets the last laugh.

Ha ha ha.

THE LAST MAN STANDING

HE SHOULD HAVE been down from the hill by now; he's been gone too long. She turns away from the window; wipes her wet hands on the tea towel. She's learned not to worry, over the years. Or rather, not to fuss. There's nothing he hates more than a fuss. But he's been gone three hours now, and still she hasn't heard the shot.

She wishes he hadn't gone today. Not today, with his hands still red-raw from digging the grave for the old dog in yesterday's freezing rain. Not today, with a heart so heavy that she's not sure his stiff old legs can carry it all the way up the hill. His heart's been heavy before, and he's found a way through it – clamped his jaw shut, straightened his bent back and set his sturdy granite chest against the wind. But she knows that this is different. Saw the difference in him this morning, when he came back from the shed and the feeding and there was only young Ruaridh to keep him company. A dog, right enough – but not the right dog. Not enough. Not the dog that he needs.

Yes, it was then that she saw – really saw, as if for the first time – that he is indeed old. Old, and all that he cares about – all that holds him together – has changed or is fading away. The old ways are all but gone now, and they'll never come back. Almost all of the crofts along this narrow lochside road have been bought up by incomers – most of them 'retired'. Retired from what? she wonders. From life? No one wants to work the land, now; they just want to sit and look out of their picture windows and stare at the water. A 'view', they call it, as if they had nothing but eyes to know this place with – and as if their eyes could ever even scratch the surface of it from where they stand. His friends and family have been dying all around him for years, and some days it seems that there'll only be him left standing at the end of the world. A crumbling saint; a reluctant relic of a way of life that's gone forever. Just like that poem she read, years ago now – about a stone statue, all that was left, dissolving in the desert at the end of everything.

He might be made of granite, but granite is a good solid rock, and it has to be said she's had a good life with him. You couldn't call him a soft man – but a quiet man, for sure. Not a man to show his emotions – but what man of his generation ever did? That's a new-fangled thing they do now: emoting at the drop of a hat. She doesn't understand it, doesn't see the need for it. Maybe if they'd had children who'd survived, she could make sense of this strange new world that was elbowing its way into all the sacred places. Maybe if there'd been grandchildren . . .

Aye, they've both carried on through losses before – for isn't that the way of all life? You gain and you lose, you lose and you gain – and it all cycles round again, year after year, as sure as the seasons and the transit of earth around sun. There have been harder losses than the death of an old dog. Calum, lost in the Falklands. Getting on for forty years ago, now. He carried on through the loss of a son; why wouldn't he carry on through the loss of a dog?

Calum. She mustn't think of Calum. She's thought enough of Calum, over the years. Hiding her pain so as not to increase his. Did he ever really feel it as she did? He would never think of telling her what he felt. And she knew better than to ask him. She understood her part in the strange bargain that was the marriage she had devised between them. There had still been things left in this world for her to learn.

She looks at the clock again: almost eleven.

She'll be worrying about him by now, he's sure of it. Ach, she tries to hide it from him, but he knows how she is. She thinks he doesn't see it: the nervous clenching of her fists; the quick smile, rapidly suppressed; the reflexive swallowing. He sees it. He sees it but what can he do? He can't protect her from it. Not from any of it. Couldn't protect her from Calum dying, all those years ago. Couldn't save her; couldn't even share her pain. Doesn't know how; never knew how. Never learned how. Too late now, to learn.

He picks his way up to the ridge, treading carefully through the boggy ground, stepping on clusters of dormant rushes to save from sinking too deeply into the wet. A hooded crow breaks into the silence with a harsh caw and he jumps. Ah, for God's sake. He never used to be jumpy. But then he never used to be slow, either. Never used to be old. He shivers, pulls the damp tweed more closely around him, inhaling the old familiar smell of wet wool and old dog.

It isn't the same, without the old dog. Nothing's the same. He got up this morning and although the young one was there, bouncing up and down with joy to see him, it wasn't the same. He hasn't the patience with the young ones any more; they need too much attention, draw too much out of you. It was the old dog that had wormed his way into his heart, over the years. The quiet dog. Stout, sturdy dog. Down to the shed in winter mornings with him to feed the sheep; up the brae behind the house to give the hens their mash. Aye, he was a fine dog. A great dog for the sheep, too.

The delicate drizzle hasn't let up since yesterday afternoon, though it's a wee bitty warmer today than it was yesterday when he dug out the grave. Eagerly accepting the sharp physical pain that coursed through his old body with every shovelful of earth. Gritting his teeth against it, setting his back to the wind. Digging in, digging on. For isn't that the way of it? Isn't that what he's always done?

Ach, but he's tired now, and old, old, old. He doesn't want to dig any more; he just wants to rest. That's how he'd always imagined it, getting old. With a few sheep for the comfort of it – just to keep him going – and an old dog beside him for warmth. Not that mad young bounding thing – and a good dog Ruaridh will turn out to be, no doubt, in his time – he just doesn't want to see another dog grow up and grow old and then die. Hasn't the heart for it. Can't bear it, if truth be told, and you bear so much, over the course of any human life. Doesn't everyone? But sometimes it seems he'll just struggle on through forever: another generation of dogs will grow old and die and still he'll be holding on.

He knows that he shouldn't complain. He has a good life. He always returns from the morning chores on the croft to a warm house and a bowl of hot porridge and the quiet comforting presence of his wife.

His wife: his beautiful, mysterious wife. It is strange to him still, that word. For he grew up without a woman in his life; his mother died when he was six, and nothing left but a houseful of silent men. And even after all the long years of marriage she is still a mystery to him. It is still a surprise to find her there waiting for him, quietly, smiling softly, trying to spare him her concerns. He has no idea where she came from, really; he has no idea what goes on inside her head.

He was out at seven-thirty, rifle slung over his shoulder and a hip flask in the pocket of his old tweed jacket. She'd tried suggesting gently over the years that he might go out in waterproofs. Well, waterproofs were fine, it seemed, for jobs around the croft – but waterproofs were not for stalking. For stalking you wore your tweed, and that was the end of it. That was how it was done, and there were too many things by far that were dying in the world now. He would keep to this one. This, at least, was within his power to keep. This one thing he would keep the way it always had been.

The way it always had been, except for the loss of the dog.

The clock strikes eleven and she jumps.

It was here that he saw the hind last month: he's sure of it. Over the ridge and down in the sheltered hollow below. And on a day like today, with no wind and only this fine drizzle, they're likely still to be up and about. He walks slowly now, and silently; eyes scanning, ears alert. Watching for a sign, rifle slung heavy over his shoulder.

He misses the old dog by his side. They'd all thought he was mad, taking a dog stalking with him. The scent alone will throw the deer off, they'd said. One whiff and they'll be away. And besides, they said, you can never get a dog to be still enough. He'll scare them off, you know it fine well. But for fifteen long years – ever since he was just out of his puppyhood – the old dog had come up the hill with him, padding softly along behind him, shadowing him. Had lain quiet beside him, paws stretched out in front, head cradled in between. Eyes open, nose twitching, ears pricking – never moving an inch. And still the deer had come.

It's the emptiness behind him that he feels, more than the cold drizzle that penetrates the old tweed and makes him shiver again. It's hard for him, now, to do this. Hard to get up the hill at seventy-seven; harder still to drag the heavy carcass of a hind down again with him. His bones are stiff and he can't lie still for hours like he used to, waiting for the deer to come into his sights. But he does his best: that's all any man can do. Sometimes it seems that stalking is the one thing that doesn't change – the only thing that stays the same. That stays true. Everything else is gone. The wild salmon have fled from the over-fished rivers and stinking loch; the ash trees are dying, and snow comes but rarely to the hills and fields.

A movement to his right – and there it is. A hind. But not just any hind: a white hind. One of his wife's strange breed. She brought them with her, when she came – from wherever it was that she came. He dips down again below the ridge, crouching, perfectly still despite the quiver in the muscles of his thighs. A clump of heather shields his head from view, and he watches her dance like a ghost through the dark green stems. He waits for a normal hind, a red – but it seems she's alone. For a moment it hangs in the balance; the hind raises her head and sniffs at the air, up towards the ridge. But there's no wind to carry the scent of the man, and the hind moves in closer and lowers her nose to graze.

He has the perfect chance of a shot now, and she'll be waiting, back home there, for the sound of the shot. But he promised he'd never kill one of her hinds. Promised her other things as well; never broke his word. Came close to it, once or twice – but if he's anything, he's a man of his word. Always has been. Unfashionable thing, now – but then nobody has a word worth keeping in this godforsaken age. It matters to him still, though, and it matters to his wife. And if it matters to her then it matters to him, for she is another thing that has always stayed true.

He can't imagine why she chose him. It's not as if there weren't other men around – men who would have been a likelier catch than him. All he had was the croft – his father dead and his brothers all gone to the city, one by one – and it had always been a hard way of life. Why would a woman like her want it? She was so beautiful – still is, with her lily-white hair and lips that are dry now, but always rose-red. She loved the land, though; understood it from the first. She walked it as if she'd known it all her life. She must have come from farming stock herself, though she never would say. Why else would she have brought the animals with her? Almost like a dowry. The strange and secretive white hinds who took to the hills from the first day; the creamy, red-eared cows who settled right into the thin-grassed fields as if they'd never dreamed of anything finer. And the long-lashed, lily-white bull who'd bellowed at them daily from the paddock down by the byre. He'd looked at them all when first they came and shook his head. How could creatures like that possibly survive this harsh northern country? They looked like summer breeds to him, in need of richer grass to flourish. And this land nourished only the sturdiest of stock: feisty, long-coated Highland cattle, or the wee grey and dun Shetlands like Roddy Alec had, down the road. But to his surprise they'd thrived. Thrived and bred, and brought in enough to keep them both fed and warm down all the years. Not rich, but rich enough, and rich enough is more than enough, in his book. Those cattle were the envy of the lochside, back in the day. Now, no one even notices them. Except to complain about cow pats on the lane when he moves them to the field next door.

He loved her, of course, right from the start. Loves her still, more than anything ever in his life. She was what held it all together; holds it all together now while the world wastes away around them. He's never actually told her, though. Couldn't ever get the words out. You need to have grown up softer, to speak them. Every time he opened his mouth they'd stuck in his throat. Men like him didn't do it, and it couldn't be helped now. He just hasn't ever been able to get the words out. He thinks she knows, though. Hopes she knows. She knows so much else. The use of meadowsweet to ease a headache; yarrow to staunch a wound. In all the years she's been with him, he's never once needed to get the vet out. She's always known what to do.

He lowers himself full length to the ground and lies flat, the rifle butt cradled against his right shoulder. He lines up his body with the gun, all pointed in a straight line towards the target. Comfortable, natural; man and weapon perfectly in tune. Just as it always has been, just as he was taught by his grandfather, all those years ago. He lines up the hind's neck in his sights, and . . .

. . . Ach. The Devil take it. The hind lifts its head again; stands poised, ready for flight, as he curses to himself quietly. Take the shot while you can, he tells himself, and be damned. She'll be waiting to hear the shot, and what does any of it matter, now? Take it while you can, this once, this last time, for you may never have another chance to walk up this hill. He closes his eyes, and for a moment it seems that he can sense it beside him: the quivering concentration of the old dog, every instinct telling it to jump up and give chase. But the old dog knew fine well when to stay, and when it was time to go. The old dog would hold itself there if it must, against its nature.

Satisfied that all is well, the hind lowers its head and sets to grazing once again.

He raises the rifle . . .

Pulls the trigger.

She hears it then: a single shot. A heavy crash that propagates; clatters down the glen like the sound of shattering glass. She clenches her fists reflexively, feels the warm worn metal of her wedding ring bite into the bony finger of her left hand. Settles herself down in the rocking chair by the fire and waits.

Waits, as she's so often waited before. And while she waits, she thinks. Thinks of the long years she's spent with this man, longer than she's ever spent with a human husband through all the long centuries of her calling. Thinks, and drifts back – back to the choice she made when he'd surprised her, dew-bathing on the flat stone down by the loch that fine Bealtaine morning, almost six decades ago now. It was an auspicious morning for such a meeting; too auspicious to write it off as chance. Well, she'd thought, as she lifted her white-frocked body up from the rock, maybe it was time again – time for her to heave herself out of the heavy waters and set her feet to the land again. Hadn't it always been so? And she'd smiled at him there, so tall and shy, so gangly and tongue-tied and stumble-footed – but she could see the trueness inside him from the start. The integrity of the land itself, as if he'd been birthed right out from its massive, stone heart.

She'd chosen well with this one; chose well the man on whom to bestow her gifts. She'd set him the usual tests, and he'd passed them – every one. He'd never struck her in anger; he'd never once spoken to anyone of where and how he found her. And he'd never raised a gun to one of her beautiful, delicate white hinds.

She doesn't unclench her fists until the creak of the gate tells her he's home. A distinctive creak; a sound that the gate makes only for him. A short creak, and firm. Others are more hesitant with the gate, open it slowly – misled, perhaps, by the years of rust that are visible on it and lend it an air of fragility.

She stands quickly, moves to the sink, picks up a tea towel. Waits until the door is open, and she hears his first step on the wooden kitchen floor before she turns, and smiles.

His face is dark – a darker shade of its customary ruddy-cheeked gauntness. She tilts her head; he shakes his. 'I missed,' he says. And turns around, and quietly closes the door behind him as he leaves the house again.

He walks back up the brae and into the field where he buried the old dog yesterday. The old dog stayed true to the end, even if it meant going against its nature. And now he can say that he has finally matched him. He'd made him a grave under the shade of an ancient plum tree; the old dog had loved that tree. He smiles to think of it: the old dog under the tree with the hens, grazing on fallen fruit. And for a moment it seems that he can see him there, head bowed with the weight of age, fur matted and tangled now, so much less shiny than when he was a puppy. The old dog wags his tail to see him and then he is gone and there is nothing but the fine drizzle and bedraggled black hens, and he lowers himself slowly down on the grave and he weeps.

He's been gone all afternoon; it's getting dark now. She wonders whether to start the tea, but doesn't want it to spoil. She hesitates. Should she go to find him? Should she interrupt him, or should she just let him be? She understands how to let him be; it's what she's always done best. But it is her own need that comes to her now; she needs to know if he will survive this. No: she needs to know *how* he will survive this. He will survive this; that's what *he* does best. And isn't that why she chose him, after all? This man who she'd imagined might know how to be worthy of her; this man who might know, in the end, how to hold true. Not just to her, but to the land. Always, and only, to the land, and the creatures who walk on it and are of it. And in all the years of their life together, he has never failed her or the land. He has never, deep in the heart of him, failed to care. She does not need to measure such things in words; she measures the truth of him in other ways. But she needs to see him, now; she needs to see how he is. She needs to know.

She pulls on her old wellies, groaning as she bends and something in her back cracks with the strain. She is old herself now in this human form; she forgets that, sometimes, too. She takes her ancient mouldering Barbour and pulls the hood tight over her head. The gate creaks behind her – a slower creak, more hesitant than his – and she walks down the path to the big shed. He'll be in there with the sheep; he always takes comfort from the sheep. They have always been at the heart of his life; he has always been a shepherd, at heart. Early spring mornings, vigilant in the chill of the lambing pens, and he'd loved every minute of it. The smell of piss and afterbirth, the smile in his eyes when she brought him a mug of tea. And a biscuit for the old dog.

He isn't in the shed.

The hens, then. He'll be in the byre with the hens.

She walks back up to the house and on along the path that leads up the brae. Opens the rickety wooden door to the old stone byre, quiet now, so as not to disturb his favourite

Orpington laying an afternoon egg. How proud he's always been of his fine-feathered rare breeds. Entering them into the Black Isle Show, selling their offspring at the mart for a fine price. But he isn't with the hens, either.

And then it comes to her: of course. He'll be with the old dog. Where else now would he be?

And it is there that she finds him, lying full length along the grave, one arm wrapped across the tiny mound as if he wants nothing more in the world than to sink through the earth, curl up and sleep alongside his old dog. The rifle rests on the ground beside him – and for a moment she stops and clutches at her throat – but then she'd have heard the shot, wouldn't she? She didn't hear a shot.

Sleeping, then?

He isn't sleeping. She bends over him, gently touches his forehead, lays her hand on his chest to feel for the heart that has beat so solidly beside her each night for fifty-eight years of marriage.

There is no beat.

She hesitates even now to disturb him, to make a fuss. She clenches her fists, goes back to the house, calls the doctor.

Sits in the rocking chair.

Waits.

The next morning, she stands in the pristine kitchen and looks around her. At the cranky old bright red Rayburn; at the fireplace now cleaned of soot and crumbling peat. At his mother's polished deal dresser, the fine old china it holds faded now, and chipped. This is, she thinks, the last kitchen she will ever see. It's the one she's loved best, of all the houses she's lived in, of all the times she came out of the loch and found it was time, after all, to set her feet to the land again. To set her concerns to the affairs of men. The seventh human house she's inhabited, the seventh human husband she's taken to her bed. She's loved every one of them – how could it be otherwise? – they're all so fragile, so easy to bruise and break. She's brought them her abundance, given each of them the chance to uncover their finest selves. But there was something more about this man. This simple man who, in the end, held true. They will not see the like of him again, in the decadent, dying days ahead.

So she will go into the loch now for the last time; she will not come again to grace the houses of men. Not of such men. The men who hold this teetering world in their blood-stained hands. She closes the dark green door behind her; she closes the creaky old gate. She walks along the gravelled path to the home field, and stares down into the dark, deep water that has sung to her daily for fifty-eight long years. Today, she will not resist its music. She calls her black sheep and her white goats to her; she calls her creamy, red-eared cows to her. She calls Angus the pure-white bull to her. The white hinds have gathered now on top of the hill; she turns, and sings them safely down. She walks the length of the field with all of her stock behind her; she passes through the old farm gate, and on down to the slippery, seaweed-strewn shores of the sea loch. Out onto the Black Shore, the threshold between this world and the other. Her world; the land beneath the waves.

The sea loch is not the way it was: the salmon farm has seen to that. She has watched its living waters turn to toxic soup. She has felt the once-revered salmon, trapped now in crowded cages of steel, grow sick and fat. Heard their songs of pain and exile; shrunk in horror from armies of lice that feed on their crooked, grey flesh. No, she will not come again to grace the houses of such men. She will take back what is hers to take, and she will go.

She stands at the edge of the loch with her feet in the lapping water, and she calls the few remaining wild fish to her. Pink salmon and flashing sea trout to her, langoustines and crabs to her. Lobster and wrasse to her, pollock and coalfish to her. Mackerel and flounder to her, slinking silver eels to her. She knows a place where they can be safe; they will not be seen again in these times. Let them come with their nets and their stinking boats; let them fetch their fine rods, their slick designer jackets and expensive waders. They will find no sustenance here. She calls the sea eagles to her; calls the old grey ladies out of the heronry by the shallows to the east. Down they'll all go – down and away; down deep where the gateway to the other place lies.

Perhaps, when the world has turned a few more times, when their remaining relics have all crumbled away into dust – perhaps then she will bathe again on the flat rock by the sea loch at Bealtaine. But she does not think she will.

The last of her men was the last man standing. And she will be the last of the fairy wives.

THE BOGMAN'S WIFE

THE DOG OTTER found me first, bottomed out in the shallows on the gravelled bed of the loch. It stood stock-still on the bank and stared. One bite and it would all have been over – but the bogman had followed its trail up the rising sun. One whiff of him and off the otter slunk. He crept up to see what it had been fishing for and stumbled, half blinded by a sudden shaft of morning light. Cloud smothered it and there I was, mercurial old me, threading a slow, silvery path through the boulders. I was tired by then. It's hard work for a sea trout, swimming this far upstream.

You think I didn't want to be caught? Don't you believe it. I wanted it all right: I was ripe for the mating. Wait too long, and my silver would turn to brown. Summer would pass, the rods would arrive, and I'd be the trout-treat on someone's table, for sure. So I flaunted my fine young tail – a flick here, a twitch there – and slowly, slowly he waded into the water. One touch of my tail, one tickle of my flank, a small scratch, and then a rub. He was born to the guddle, that one, and how I preened, how still I stayed, till he guddled me all the way out of the water and into his arms.

He wasn't a man to put them back, not him. I saw the wanting in his eyes; I saw the need, the deadweight of it pressing him down into the peat. He was a big man; hair thick and black as a sod of fresh-cut turf, eyes brown as the shadow of a cloud easing its way across a sunny winter bog. He was a hungry man, and I was the meal he'd been waiting for all his life. He carried me home, rough tweed jacket scrubbing at my skin, and I shed my scales one by one.

He carried me into a house he'd built himself, from blocks of grey granite hewn from the wrinkled old mountains to the east. And there I stood, landed now, saltwater to fresh, water to earth I came. Skin white as the roiling sheets on the tidal wave of his bed; hair silver as moonlight striking a quartz stone in a lonely moorland stream.

'Marry me,' I said; and he did.

They said it would never last, that I was a fish out of water, and him – well, he was a hard one, wedded to rock and peat. He wasn't much of a man for talking, but then I hadn't much of a tongue myself. We rubbed along well enough. I couldn't tell you exactly what he did with his days out in the hills, but he kept us in fuel and food, and that was good enough for me.

When my own work in the house was done I would take myself out to the moor. It was the simple wetness of it that hooked me, the manifold forms that water could take. The sinking bog suited me best, for no bog could sink me. I'd dive right down through the bright green grass, shudder with joy at the icy black water cradled in its bottomless bowl of peat.

I'd dance across the quaking bog, light as a bubble in the places where no one else could safely tread. I never went to the loch, though. Somehow, it made me sad.

I began to leave him on the day I understood that it wasn't so much me he'd wanted, as a glimpse of an underwater world which was lighter and shinier than his own. On a sunny Sunday in the middle of June, he coaxed me along to his church. Heaviness and sin, damnation and misery – that was what they worshipped in that cold stone house. Prissy old preachers with biblical beards, crow-like in black woollen suits. Build your houses with their backs to the shore, they exhorted, for the sea is filled with irreligious things. Turn your faces away from the Earth, they demanded, for the Earth's beauty is a sinful thing. And don't lift your eyes to the sky, they said; you're not worthy to look on the face of God. When their spittle-filled sermon denounced the sins of the flesh, he extracted his hand from mine.

I laughed at him then; I laughed at them all. I saw the chains with which they'd willingly shackled their hearts; I perceived the prisons they'd voluntarily made of their souls. I laughed in the face of their god, and I walked out of that god's house for good. For good, for god, for my god speaks with the voice of a wave; he lives in a house which has no doors. It is hate that they preach from their bitter pulpits, but the god of the loch sings love.

I left him for the first time on the day he went to the loch in the morning and later brought home a trout. Threw her down on the kitchen table, browning body dull and thin. Slit her open right in front of me, and the thick clot of orange eggs spilled out of her belly and onto the cold flagged floor. He flung down his knife and spat in the fire as he strode away. Chips, he said. We'll have it with chips. For tea.

Me, I had other fish to fry. I gathered up the eggs and carried them down to the loch. I took them home and laid them in the arms of the shiny god of the waters. The tears I shed were brackish, and a sea-longing entered my heart. I slept on a bed of soft sedge, and when I found my way home in the morning I found he'd let the fire go out.

I left him for good when he fell for a woman carved from the same stone. A great lumbering hulk of a woman, the kind their preachers preferred. I saw him gawp at her big breasts, I saw him assess the width of her hips. She was made for it, he could see it right away. Fashioned for fruitfulness, given by God – she'd hatch him the sons I never could. She hooked him as he turned back down to his lie, and I watched as she reeled him in. She'd worked as a herring girl back on the mainland, cheating fish of their skins. Had a little house of her own on the proceeds; let him in now most nights when he came licking at her window. A professional gutter, that one; I shuddered when I looked in her eyes. His guddle and her gutting – he must have thought they were made for each other. I scented her gansey which reeked of blood and smoke, and remembered what it is to be prey.

*

I left the peat-stained sheets and the smouldering embers of his turf fire; I left the cracked bedrock of his heart. I left him clues to trace my path; riddles he'd never be able to answer.

Follow the snipe's flight, follow the otter spraint;
follow me down to the water.
Follow the wind's bite, follow the fish-taint;
follow the sea-king's daughter.
Follow me down to the water-lily bed,
to the place where bogbean binds me.
You may follow for a while in my footsteps, there –
but you will not find me.

I was last seen on the black shore, on the sand by the glittering loch. I tore off my clothes and abandoned my shoes. A shimmer of air, a flash of silver, and I was the one that got away.

I came to myself again in the chill of the gravel beds; I remembered who I was. A cold fish, for sure. As I swam for the surface, the scales fell away from my eyes. So I breached the still and holy waters; I beached myself in the blackness of the bog. I raised my eyes to their storm-strewn heaven, my fists to the clouds which covered the face of their sour and skulking god. If it was God they wanted, it was God they would have. An eye for an eye, a gut for a gut. I took a fish knife to the house of the fish-wife. When I stepped over her threshold, all the candles in the house blew out.

*

It was the cat who found me first. I stood naked on his doorstep, and shivering, pondweed streaming from my hair. Neither fish I was then nor fowl, but the cat screeched anyway; the dogs began to bark and soon he was there at the door. I opened my hand and offered him the gift I'd brought; he grew a little green around the gills. But I had treated it gently, the egg that had been growing in her soft, full belly. I'd laid it out on her best gutting apron, tied it carefully in a bow fashioned from a braid of her long red hair.

He wasn't a man to weep – not that one – but I can tell you he wept then. Tears black as a bog's blood, oil-streaks slickening his stubbled cheek. I lifted a cold hand to his hot face; I winked a glassy eye.

Never mind, I said; there are plenty of fish in the sea. We can have this one with chips, I said. For tea.

FOXFIRE

I SAW THE FOX first; she was mine from the beginning. A flash of red, like lifeblood, on the white-wintered fringe of the wood. So vivid she was, so tangible. The epitome of all that was wild and free. My heart sprang suddenly to life again and almost burst; I thought I had never seen anything so beautiful. So beautiful, so alive, that I cried out before I could stop myself. The fox stopped, turned, looked directly at me. Our eyes locked, the warmth of her amber melting my cold blue ice, and in that moment I was lost.

I began to go to the wood each day, hoping to catch a glimpse of her. Most days she would come. She knew I was there, and it didn't seem to worry her. She allowed me to watch her, and sometimes she let me follow for a while, looking back every now and then as if to make sure that I was still with her. Sometimes she would lead me out of the wood, all the way through to the low hills and wide plains beyond. I would rest there awhile to catch my breath, and watch her run and play and roll in the snow. On those days I would return home content but weary; it had been a long time since I'd pushed my body so far. I'd forgotten what breathlessness felt like, or the bite of winter wind whipping up a storm in my hair. I'd forgotten what it was to be alive. And what I remembered, I didn't much care for at all.

I began to bring her food. I broke it into fragments which I would throw onto the ground, taking one step back, and then another, so that she would learn to come to me. But she always stopped short. She'd make a sudden sharp dart to snatch up the morsel I'd just put down – and then she would scuttle away, looking over her shoulder as if to tease, pink tongue dangling out of a wide-mouthed, sharp-toothed grin. She'd always manage somehow to make me smile, and that wasn't so easy to do in those days. After my last miscarriage – the third – the laughter had bled right out of me along with the dead foetus. With every child lost over the years, I'd lost more of myself. In the months leading up to that winter in our dark, northern wood, I didn't know who I was any more. I didn't even know why I should care.

One day, I caught the fox napping on top of a dry fallen trunk in the middle of the woods. I crept up quietly to her and reached out my hand. Her bright golden eyes opened. Just for a few seconds she let me touch the soft fur on the top of her head, and then she leapt up and ran away. I put my hand to my nose, and breathed in the faintest rank, wild smell of her. Spirit of fox, sucked up inside me; seeping through the walls of my lungs, inhabiting my flesh and inspiriting my bones.

I didn't just love the fox, you see – I wanted to be her. Longed for it, as I had never longed for anything in my life. To be sleek and fast; to be beautiful and fierce, feral and unconstrained. To run wherever I wanted to run, to make my dark home in the belly of the fecund earth, to hunt at dawn in the wildness of a moonlit wood. So very long since I had wanted anything, other than oblivion. I wasn't naive, though: I knew it was a hard life. The winters were cold, and food was scarce. There was always the threat of a farmer's gun, the fear of a hunting dog, or an iron trap to break and tear. But some chances must be taken, if you want to live fully. She lived fully, my fox, and I envied her with all my heart. I wanted to dance with her, sister or lover, across the snow-clad vastness of this land. Together, we'd create the Northern Lights. For that is what foxes do – racing over the fells, whipping up the snow with their tails, the friction of it sending up sparks into the midnight sky. This is what makes the aurora's glow. *Revontulet*, we call it: foxfire.

Each day, I stayed a little longer in the woods; I returned with flushed cheeks and bright eyes, for my senses were slowly beginning to come alive again. My husband began to wonder what I was doing. And why wouldn't he? For months I'd spent my days sitting alone and still, enshrouded in the dark mustiness of the small, neat bedroom which was supposed to have belonged to our child. 'Oh,' I said, with a swift shake of my head. 'It's nothing. I just want to be outside, that's all. I like the fresh, crisp air. It makes me feel good.'

But he must have grown suspicious, for one morning he crept out after me, and followed me into the wood. So silently did he tread that I didn't know he was there till the fox came bounding out of the trees to greet me – and then froze, her glowing eyes firmly fixed on something behind me. She didn't even acknowledge me; she just turned tail and ran. I knew at once that it was him. I lifted my nose and sniffed, caught the faint scent of the pine resin which always permeated his clothes. A twig cracked underfoot as he faded slowly into the trees and made his way back to the house. Did he imagine I wouldn't see his tracks? Did he really think so little of me? Or had he simply, by then, ceased to care?

We did not speak that day of what had happened, but the next morning he arose before I did. He was out of the door and into the wood before I had managed even to fumble my way down the stairs. It was my turn then to follow, torn between sorrow and fury. She was my fox – *mine*, and his uncovering of my secret, his usurping of my place, felt like a violation.

Somehow I knew she would come for him. Somehow I knew it, and she came. She was just that kind of fox. She slunk silently through the woods, belly low and nose to the ground, as if tracking the scent of newly found prey. And then she saw him, and I saw him see her. I heard him catch his breath; I heard a faint, barking laugh. Then it was no longer a fox standing there before him in the woods, but a woman. A beautiful woman with red-gold hair, eyes amber as the fossilised heart of a tree.

I saw my husband fall. And I fled.

I followed him when he slipped out again the next morning; of course I followed him. I followed him as he confidently made his way through a thicket, and on into an older, wilder part of the wood which I had never discovered. And, peering through the cracked windows of a well-hidden, ramshackle cabin in a secret tree-dark glade, I saw what I should never have had to see. My husband, in a dusty, candlelit room with a fire burning brightly in its hearth. A flash of red hair falling down the length of her back; two bodies stretched out on a mattress covered with furs. And, hanging over the edge of the bed, a fox tail.

My heart clattered loudly in my chest as dread overtook me. *Huldra*. She was a huldra! Couldn't he see it? Didn't he care? I had heard the stories; we had all heard them as children – stories told to make a child think twice before wandering alone into the wildwood. When you're face to face with a huldra, they said, she presents herself as a woman who is beautiful beyond belief. So beautiful that no man can resist her. But if you see her from behind, it is clear that she is something else entirely. Her back is carved out, and her body cavity is empty – and what's more, she has the full, red tail of a fox. The huldra, they told us, was the ultimate seductress: she would gladly offer herself to any man who stumbled into her woods. But the place where her heart should have been was hollow. She wouldn't think twice about killing those men who were unable to satisfy her, or those of whom she had grown bored. What would this huldra do to my husband when she was finished with him? And without him, faithless creature though it seemed he was, what would I then become?

I backed away from the window; I closed my eyes and breathed slow and deep to quiet my pounding heart. Then I ran away home, and made my plan.

*

He came home in the late afternoon, elated and trying (failing) to hide it. He smelled (did he know it?) of fox. It was a long time since I had seen his eyes shine so. I mixed a strong sleeping draught into his bedtime drink, and, after a sleepless night gauging the depth of his snores, I crept out of the house at first light and retraced the path to the cabin.

She was there, waiting for him, stretched out under the furs, a log fire blazing again in the rusty old grate. She didn't move when I burst through the door; she simply raised an elegantly slanted red-gold eyebrow and smiled. She didn't seem especially surprised to see me. The room smelled rank, and wild. I looked into her beautiful golden eyes and tears welled up in my own. I swallowed hard and clenched my fists, not so much then mourning my marriage as mourning the fox I had loved – the fox I had thought of as my only friend.

At last, I found my voice. 'So you're a huldra,' I said to her, the words catching in a throat that was hoarse with fear and sorrow. 'A huldra! I've heard all the stories about things like you. You're not a woman at all – you're not even a fox. Only some devilish creature who wishes to do harm. Will you kill my husband when you're done with him, when he no longer satisfies you? Will you kill me too, for discovering your secret?' And, sobbing, I pulled out the sharp silver knife I had hidden in the deep pockets of my grey woollen coat.

But she only smiled again, revealing the sharp white teeth which protruded from her blood-red gums. 'You shouldn't believe all the fairy stories you're told,' she said. 'And not all of us are what we seem. Perhaps not even you.' Then she stood

– red of hair, white of skin, long-limbed and heartbreakingly beautiful. She turned around and began to walk over to the farthest dark corner of the room. And as she did so, I gasped – for her naked back above the foxtail was sleek, and entirely whole.

What could I do but let my knife clatter to the floor, and follow? The fox-woman came to a halt in front of a tall wooden wardrobe with a mirror which stretched the full length of its door. She took a candlestick from a nearby table, lit the candle, and held it up between us. 'Stand with your back to the mirror,' she said, and I did. 'Now turn your head, and look, and we will see which one of us is empty.'

I stretched my neck and looked over my own shoulder into the mirror. I looked, and I saw, and then I screamed. For in the place where my back should be was a huge gaping hole, hollow as a long-rotted tree trunk.

I sat trembling by her fire and sipped at the broth she gave me; I felt as if I were drinking down the spirit of the forest itself. It tasted of wood sorrel and wild mushrooms; it was laced with lichen and shoots of spruce. She did not speak another word to me, but she sat with me there at her hearth as the broth opened my throat, and I wept.

I wept for the children who were lost to me, for the empty years I'd wasted and the strong, healthy body I'd shunned. For the desolate woman I'd become, with her hollow centre and closed-down heart, and the husband whose clumsy but loving efforts at comfort I'd always turned aside. I wept for both of us, each locked into our own fatal sorrow, trapped inside our own lonely skins. It had taken a fox to show us what we needed. To show us what we were missing, and how very much we had lost.

When eventually I lifted my hands from my sodden face, she was gone. And on the simple wooden stool across from me where she had sat, was a fox tail.

I lifted it in my hands are pressed it to my face; I inhaled the wild, rank smell of fox. I stroked the soft plush fur, let its vulpine spirit fill me to the brim. I wrapped the tail like a scarf around my neck, and I went home. To my husband, and the tattered remains of my life.

She never came again to my husband. He mourned her, of course, for a while. But when I came fox-tailed to our bed and opened my arms to him, when I pulled his hair and bit his neck with sharpening white teeth, when I tangled and tore the sheets with sharp-clawed pleasure – I was the one he began to seek out in the wild heart of the wood.

I am learning to become full again; the forest is showing me how. I go there each day, and I roll among leaves on the damp, mossy floor. I burrow into root balls and talk to trees, and I am beginning to understand what they whisper to me in return.

Yes, I go each day into the wildwood, and sometimes I catch a glimpse of red-gold fur through the trunks. Sometimes, waking in the dark of night, I hear a vixen screaming deep in the heart of the forest. I am glad that she is there, living her own wild life. I am glad that I knew her; I am glad for the hard lesson that she taught me. But I will not follow her again.

Now, I have my own wild-pawed path, and the power of the wood is remaking me. For when last I crept out to the cabin in the clearing and examined myself again in its mirror of truth, the hole at the heart of me was almost closed.

MEETING BABA YAGA

I SAW HER AD in *Resurgence* magazine the day I came back from my first time at the Glastonbury Festival. I was trying to cope with a magic mushroom hangover, and still having flashbacks. It hadn't been a bad trip, but the talking mailboxes were a bit weird. 'Journey to the Bone House', the ad said. 'Shapeshifting a speciality.' I'd recently done a weekend course in shamanic journeying, but it hadn't felt like the real thing. One of the teachers came from Peru, or somewhere weird like that, and I couldn't understand a word he said. I wanted to connect properly with my power animal, and this looked just the job.

It was a long way to go, but frankly I needed a holiday. I was feeling the call to adventure, I suppose you could say. Things at work were dragging me down, and I really needed to spend some more time on my own self-development. I'd been trying to find myself for two years now, and if the Russian woods were the next step on the Heroine's Journey of my life, then the Russian woods it would be. I felt as if I'd done all the right things, so far – moved down to Totnes, read everything from Louise Hay to Deepak Chopra, subscribed to *Kindred Spirit*. I'd dabbled in Buddhism and Wicca; done a course on past-life regression – the lot. But somehow it just wasn't happening for me. *The Secret* didn't give up its secret. The universe just wasn't aligning, you know?

So: a week in the taiga it was. It'd probably be a bit fresh there in early October, but it'd make a nice change from my usual yearly yoga retreats on Skyros. I packed my angel cards; I packed my portable altar. I packed my newly minted copy of *The Power of Now*. And away I went.

It was the human skulls on top of the fenceposts that gave the place away. Though I have to say, it wasn't *quite* what I'd been expecting. Every one of them had a candle inside, eye sockets all lit up, grinning away in the late afternoon gloom like some half-crazed band of jack-o'-lanterns. Not exactly your average turnip. So a bit of internal reprocessing was required. If she was going to turn out to be some weird Russian goth, then I could go with that . . . maybe. Because then I saw that the fenceposts were actually bones. And the gate looked like it was made out of a ribcage. It had a skeleton's hand for a latch and a lock made of clacking teeth. Oh, come on! I thought to myself. What was this – some kind of oddball, super-boreal Hallowe'en-themed Disneyland? But then it got worse: I saw the house. If you could call it that. More like a madwoman's hut. It seemed like a regular sort of log cabin until you looked down at the ground – and then you saw it was perched on a pair of giant chicken feet! I kid you not – *chicken feet*!

'What the f—' I began, but my companions just sniggered. We'd all met up at the airport to share a ride, because apparently this place was sort of 'out of the way'. *Out of the way?* It had taken us three hours through the forest in a clapped-out old minibus with a driver who looked like Igor out of one of those old Dracula movies, and any minute now I was expecting the bats to come swooping out of the trees. I was knackered, and this was frankly freaking me out. It was all right for them; they'd already told me they'd been here before – well, four of them had, anyway. Except for me, and an Irishwoman called Deirdre. And Deirdre was turning out to be one of those really irritating people who just take everything in their stride. And who stand about grinning inanely while Rome's burning and the barbarians are gathering at the gates, you know? Saying, 'Ah sure, we'll work it out.'

So anyway. We all climb out of the minibus, stagger a bit as we try to get our arms and legs moving again in the cold, rub our eyes – and then all of a sudden, all these blood-curdling screeches start coming from the house. No, I'm not making all this up! It sounded like a klaxon going off; it sounded like the end of the world. I almost wet myself; I'd been dying for a pee for the past hour, but old Igor wasn't exactly the kind of bloke you asked. I looked at the house again, and it was shaking. Moving from side to side on its stupid bony chicken legs, shimmying in time with its own shrieks. And then I realised something else strange about it: I couldn't see any doors or windows; couldn't see any way we could possibly get in. That's assuming we'd ever want to. And I can tell you, it wasn't anything I was counting on wanting right now. If all this seriously screwy malarkey carried on for much longer, I was getting back in that minibus and scuttling off down the road with Igor. I'd cosy up with my power animal some other time, thank you very much. Preferably in Totnes.

Then some skinny cow called Carol from Hartlepool – from *Hartlepool*! – says, matter of fact as you please, as if screeching, dancing houses are just ten a penny in the dark industrial north-east, says it will only stop when the right words are spoken. 'Yeah, right,' I say to her knowingly, rolling my eyes. 'And what words might THEY be?' But she just shakes her head at me, rolls her eyes in turn, then walks through the gate and starts talking to the house. As you do. But by this time, I've given up expecting sense. I'm not entirely sure I'm not still in the minibus, locked into some funky travel-fuelled nightmare – but if I am, that weekend workshop I did on lucid dreaming in Findhorn isn't helping at all. I've absolutely no idea how to take back control of this one.

'Turn your back to the forest,' Carol says to the house. 'Turn your front to me.' And bugger me if the house doesn't stop its pantomime right away. Slowly, it revolves, swings around to face us, and now, finally, I can see the windows and the door. They were all on the other side; wouldn't you just know it. There are ludicrously ornate carvings around the windows, all picked out in red and blue and yellow, like a house right out of some silly old fairy tale. I suppose; I never was one for fairy tales myself. Could never really see the point of them as a kid. I preferred reading about things that were real, you know? All that stupid stuff about handsome princes and fairy godmothers and wicked old witches in the woods . . .

Well, anyway. All of a sudden the front door bursts open with a crash – and there she is. The reason we're all here.

'Hello,' she says. 'I'm the Baba. But you all can call me Babs.'

What was she like? I don't really know where to begin. She was everything and nothing; she was perfectly normal and perfectly strange. One minute, your average little old lady, bustling about the kitchen making tea. The next minute, she'd swivel sharply to face you, and everything in the room would suddenly grow still. The air would tingle, and the faintest feeling of pins and needles would set up a prickling in your fingers and toes. Your hair wanted nothing more in the world than to stand on end. She was a tiny little thing, but the shadow she cast was always huge. And it's funny, now I come to think of it: she cast a shadow even when the sky was overcast, or when there was no direct light source at all.

When she opened the door to us, I couldn't see anything but a silhouette, and all I can tell you about that silhouette is that it . . . changed. For a few seconds it would look like the outline of a perfectly normal human being, and then it would shimmer and shift, and you'd swear that a bear was standing in that doorway instead of a little old woman. So I was still hesitating, I can tell you, but the other three acolytes had followed Carol through the gate and now the lot of them had disappeared into the house. Deirdre and me hung back a bit, but when I looked to her for a bit of moral support, all she did was wink at me. 'Sure, you're all right out, so,' she said, or something equally – and incomprehensibly – Irish. 'I'm betting the first thing she'll do is offer us a nice hot drop, and then you'll be just grand.' It took me three whole days to figure out that a 'hot drop' meant a cup of tea. Why she couldn't just say that, I really don't know.

So. I looked around a bit, playing for time. Igor was unloading our bags; he dropped them a good distance away from the fence, and there was something in the way he wasn't looking at the house that made it very clear that nothing in the world was going to induce him to go through that gate. And then, having managed to accomplish the entire journey without saying a single word to anyone, he got right back into the bus and drove off down the track. No idea what all that was about; he didn't even ask to be paid. So, when Deirdre headed off into the house as well, there was nothing for me to do but follow.

The front door opened right into a large, bright yellow kitchen. It wasn't your average kitchen, I can tell you, and I began to realise there and then that there wasn't going to be very much that was average about this whole freaking 'experience'. The room was dominated by an absolutely enormous stove, built of white-painted bricks or concrete or something similar, that stretched the entire length of one wall. It had an oven that must have been a good six feet wide – no, I'm really not exaggerating! – and a sort of a seat built into it on one side. On that seat was a big cushion, and on that cushion was perched a particularly disagreeable-looking black cat. Yes, I know; I really wanted to roll my eyes at this point, as well. If it hadn't been for the fact that Carol and her cronies had all been here before, I'd be beginning to wonder whether someone wasn't seriously taking the piss. Setting us up, you know? But anyway: on the other side of the kitchen was an equally enormous dark wooden table, with a long, high-backed bench along the wall, and simple wooden chairs around two other sides. On the third side was a huge, intricately carved wooden chair that looked for all the world like a throne. There was a dresser, crammed with brightly painted dishes, and a giant ceramic sink that you could have had a bath in. The room smelled of smoky wood and freshly baked bread – with an undercurrent of very mature, probably seriously blue cheese. Stinkingly Stilton-esque. Grotesquely Gorgonzola.

Well, good old Babs stands in the middle of the room, puts her hands on her hips, and looks us all up and down. I look her up and down as well. She's all got up in some ridiculous bright red, long velvet frock, with an embroidered apron over the top of it which really needs a good wash. What seems like an awful lot of steel-grey hair is bundled up into a shaggy bun that looks for all the world as if a crow or three has been nesting in it. She's wearing Doc Martens on her feet, and a pair of thinly striped hand-knitted socks that don't even pretend to match. The merriment in her eyes is quite at odds with the curious sharpness of her teeth.

'A wery, WERY big velcome to all you girrrrrls,' she says, in this comically thick Russian accent, like something out of a really bad Hollywood movie, or like that funny little bloke in the original *Star Trek* – what was his name? Chekov, that's it – and I'm, like, this cannot be happening! 'Jou must all go and brrring in your begs. And zen we will hef somesing to eat.' Then, all of a sudden, she points right at me and bursts out into some mad cackle – I suppose everything I'm thinking must be showing on my face. She drops the whole act in a flash, chucks me a wink, and says, in a perfect take-off of Deirdre – who hasn't even opened her mouth yet – 'Along with a nice hot drop.'

So yeah, we had the works: a fine Russian brew from a silver-plated samovar, and a platter of unidentifiable but very tasty sweet things. The only thing that bothered me was that so much of the food was meat. You are what you eat, after all, and I've never been comfortable eating animals. Usually at these things there's a vegan option. I know tofu isn't to everyone's taste, but Quorn have a nice selection of fake meat for the diehards. But yeah, you're right. Maybe they don't do Quorn in the taiga.

She didn't say much that first night, and neither did anyone else. But the Fabulous Four were obviously completely in awe of her. Gaped at her like she was the goddess, or something. Her favourite seemed to be some young woman called Lisa. She lived in Manchester now, but was originally, she said, from Russia. Not too far down the road from Babs's place, as it happened. I found out later she was married to the descendant of some Russian aristocrat. I didn't think they had those any more, since Stalin. Maybe they all came out of the woodwork after glasnost. Beats me. The other two were like Tweedledum and Tweedle-bloody-dee. Neither of them spoke unless the other one did, and then they both spoke at once. Debbie and Dora from Shepherd's Bush. I never did learn to tell them apart.

So anyway, while we were eating, I asked her about the schedule and format for the week ahead. Didn't seem like an unreasonable question; I just wanted to know where the workshop room was, and when we'd have our alone time. Mealtimes – that kind of thing. How the wi-fi worked; there wasn't any mobile signal, I'd already checked. Well – you'd have thought I'd asked whether it would be okay to take a shit in the corner of the kitchen. She raised those steely grey eyebrows at me, looked down her big old hooked nose, and said, with a pseudo-aristocratic sneer, 'What – you think you're at kindergarten or somesing? You want me to dress you in mornings, as well? Tell you when to use toilet, when to brush your teef?' The Fabulous Four sniggered; even Deirdre grinned. I went red as a beetroot and, I can tell you, if I'd been back home in Totnes I'd have walked out right there and then and told her to stuff her shapeshifting speciality up her bum. But I very clearly wasn't in Totnes any more.

It was all downhill from there, really.

After we'd had our tea, she announced that it was bedtime, and stood up to show us to our rooms. Nothing like a bit of good old Soviet totalitarianism, eh? Democracy certainly didn't seem to be part of her scene. But it was pitch-black outside now, and although I couldn't see a clock anywhere – and we couldn't seem to find a watch that worked – it must've been getting quite late. She opened one of the two doors which faced each other on opposite sides of the kitchen; the other one, she said, was 'forbidden'. That was her side of the house, and if we went into any one of the rooms down that corridor, chances were the floor would open up in front of us, and we'd plunge to a very unpleasant death. That was if we went through the blue door, she said – or was it the red? No, if we opened the red door, a guillotine would be displaced which would fall down and rapidly remove our heads. I asked whether we had to wait for Shakin' sodding Stevens to show up and tell us what would happen if we all went a-knocking on the green door, but nobody else thought that was funny. Bunch of weirdos, the lot of them. Yeah, maybe they were all just a bit too young. Old Shaky pretty much died out in the nineties, didn't he, when you come to think of it.

So we all traipsed through the door we were allowed to go through, and I swear the place was like the Tardis. There was no way that many rooms could fit into the footprint of the little wooden hut we'd seen from outside. But by this stage I was so wiped out I didn't care. I just wanted to crawl into bed and sleep for a week. We were all sharing rooms: Carol with Lisa, Tweedledee and Tweedledum together, and then me and Deirdre right at the end of the corridor. There were two bathrooms, and Deirdre and me stuck our heads in to have a peek at the facilities. They smelled of hot pinewood and birch leaves. So Deirdre said, anyway. I wouldn't know a birch leaf if it hit me in the face. I was just happy to know there was running water.

The bedroom was nice enough. Two single beds built into sort of alcoves, with bright blue embroidered curtains so you could really shut the world out if you wanted. Then old Grandmother Stasi there tells us that all the lights will go out in half an hour and that will be that till morning. 'Sleep well,' she says, and she smiles, but I can't help thinking that something about the way she bares those sharp teeth makes it sound like a threat. And bugger me, the lights do go off in half an hour. And there's no way of getting them back on again. She must've turned the electricity off at the mains.

What do you mean, was there mains electricity right there bang in the middle of the forest?

Oh, I see. Well then, she must've had a generator somewhere. I never saw one, but then . . .

Whatever. So that was that. End of day one. Welcome to Russia, and welcome to the local lunatic asylum. Still, I slept quite well. Though every time I came to during the night, all I could hear was the sound of Deirdre snoring and Nosferatu the cat meowing and scratching at the door.

No, that wasn't the cat's name. It was probably Ivan, or something.

Did I let it in?

Not on your nelly.

Well, if I gave you a running commentary on everything that happened that week we'd be here all day, and I've got to get back for the team meeting this afternoon, or Spike'll have my neck. So I'd better speed up a little, get to the most important bits.

She left us to our own devices at breakfast. Plonked an enormous pan of porridge down on the table, along with some kind of brown bread and honey. The coffee was far too strong, but beggars can't be choosers, I suppose; she just glared when I asked her for decaf. So that first morning I was just trying to get a feel for what was going on here, but the Fabulous Four weren't exactly forthcoming.

'You really need to just chill out and let it happen,' says Carol.

'Yeah, but let *what* happen?' I say. 'I've no idea what we're supposed to be doing here. And what kind of shaman is she, anyway?' I mean, she didn't even have a rattle or a drum. Carol just shook her head again. If she didn't watch herself, it was going to fall off. Snooty cow.

So that first day, all we do is go into the forest. We're going to collect mushrooms, apparently. Well, la-di-bloody-da. My spirits rise for a minute when I think she might mean magic mushrooms, but it turns out we're gathering brown ceps for our tea. Off we trot, like a passel of peasants, armed with dinky little baskets and ridiculously large knives. It was weird, though, walking into the forest from the clearing where her house is. It felt alive, somehow. As if the forest was a great big mouth, and it was opening to swallow you up. There were no paths; we just had to trust that she knew where she was going and make sure we kept up with her. But we kept hearing crackling in the distance, as if someone or something was treading on broken-off branches, and I got quite jumpy in the end.

'So,' I say to Carol, 'are there animals in these woods?'

'Of course there are animals,' she says. 'Moose, wolverines, wild boar, bear . . .'

'Hang on a minute,' I say. 'Bear?'

'Brown bear,' says Carol, with satisfaction.

'In these woods?' I squeak. 'Brown fucking bears?' And I make a BIG mental note to check my travel insurance when we got back; I wanted to be very sure it would cover any accidental maulings. You really can't be too careful, can you, when you're in proper foreign climes?

Well, we finally found the mushrooms – stalks like tree trunks; I could see why we had the big knives now – and set about picking them. But I was really irritated by the whole thing, I can tell you. 'When are we going to do some proper work?' I whisper to Lisa. 'Something other than gathering mushrooms?'

'This isn't about *doing*,' she says. 'It's about *being*. You're supposed to watch her. See how she is, here in the forest. Learn from her.'

'Learn *what*, though?' I say, frustrated. 'I didn't come all this way for a mushroom foraging course!'

'What can you be thinking?' she says. 'Do you actually *do* thinking at all?' And then she tosses her shiny blonde hair and flounces off to pick in another patch.

Well, really. I mean, there was no call for that.

But I tried, then – I honestly did. After all, I'd paid a small fortune to be here. I needed to extract something from the experience. So I watched her. But all *she* seemed to be doing was watching the forest. And talking to things. She talked to crows quite a lot. 'What is she saying to them?' I ask Deirdre. 'And what's the point?'

'Crows know things,' says Deirdre, helpfully. 'In Ireland we have this crow goddess called the Morrígan. She's really fierce, so. Flies over battlefields and gnaws on the bones of the dead. That sort of thing.'

'Lovely,' I mutter, and walk away with a mock-vomit. Jesus. Sometimes I thought Deirdre was a little bit slow, you know?

She was always talking about things like fairy hills and fairy woods and fairy fucking forts, and it was all beginning to get on my tits. Well, I decided there and then that I was never going to come on one of these things again unless someone like you was with me, so I could have a proper conversation with someone halfway normal.

So anyway, eventually Babs turns to us and starts up her preaching again. 'Ze forest is a community,' she says. 'Pine talks to oak, oak talks to birch. Birch whispers to crow, who passes it on to grey owl. Deer comes along, hears what's what from bear. Bear heard it all from mushrooms, whose network goes to root of things. Listen – can you hear it? How, when you are silent, and open ears and heart, everything speaks to you? How stream sings and wind whispers?' Well, I can get that kind of bullshit from a poetry book; I don't need to listen to it live from some Russian version of Granny Weatherwax channelling Mary bloody Oliver. Any minute now she'd be off like Mary, waxing lyrical about the earth remembering us and taking us back tenderly, when actually it was absolutely bloody perishing and I was freezing my arse off. What I wanted was to connect with my power animal, not muse poetically on the social networking capabilities of a brown cep. I don't think that really illuminates my soul's purpose in this particular incarnation, do you?

Oh, I just stopped listening at that stage. What was the point?

But Babs had clearly tuned into the fact that I wasn't having it. Turns her beady black eyes on me and 'Beryl,' she snaps – she knew perfectly well my name was Cheryl, but all week she insisted on calling me Beryl – 'there are many portals in the woods. How will you find them if you don't learn to see?'

And I think, but don't actually say, that if I could *learn to see* the portal that'd whisk me back home to Totnes, I'd be off out of this loony bin in a flash.

What was really irritating is that she made us do the housework as well. No, I'm not having you on! I didn't pay to spend a week skivvying, either, but she wasn't a woman to be argued with, that one. Carol was to do the dusting; she handed me a broom. Didn't even have a vacuum cleaner, FFS.

Well, I suppose she sees the look on my face, because she sets off on one of her moralising little lectures, silly old git. 'It is work that transforms us,' she announces. 'Work that transforms base metal into gold. Learn to apprentice yourself to the work, and you will reap rewards of your own becoming.' Yeah, right. Reap the rewards of becoming a glorified skivvy – can't think of anything I'd rather do, I'm sure. 'I am teaching how to keep your house in order,' she drones on. 'How to sort wheat from chaff.' And then, while we're running around working our fingers to the bone, she plonks herself down on that comfortable hot-seat by the stove – Nosferatu must've gone out on one of his daily bloodsucking expeditions – and starts telling us some ridiculous old story about some princess or other who was given a task by a wicked stepmother, or wicked witch – buggered if I could keep track of it all – which involved splitting a ginormous heap of mixed grains into piles of the same kind, which of course she can't possibly do, and then she's nice to a bunch of starving mice or something and so they help her sort the grains . . . Everyone else was lapping it up but I just closed my ears and started humming 'Heigh-Ho' out of spite. You know, that song from *Snow White and the Seven Dwarfs*? The one where they're all coming home from work, or something, and seem to be really happy about it?

Well, anyway.

Once we'd done the kitchen she took us outside, and round the back of the house there was this great big contraption that looked for all the world like a mortar – you know – those thick bowl thingies you grind spices in – and next to it, propped up against the wall, was something that looked like a giant pestle. She made us polish it every day, like it was some kind of valuable vintage car or something. Then in the evenings, after dinner, we had a sort of 'Ask Aunty Babs' session. She would sit down on her big carved wooden throne at one end of the table and 'So,' she would say. 'Ask me anything.'

Well, the first evening, I wasn't sure how that was supposed to work. What if everyone started asking questions all at once? Where was the structure here, anyway? 'Isn't there a talking stick?' I ask, and she stares at me for a minute, gets up out of her chair, walks over to the stove, lifts up the lid of a wooden box which sat next to it, and comes back with a sodding bone. Yes, honestly! – a bone! – which she hands to me with a bow, like she's presenting me with a precious gift, or something. Oh, very fucking cunning, I thought, and snatched it out of her hand.

I suppose she imagined that was funny; everyone else did, anyway. Cackled themselves silly. Bitches. I wouldn't have minded, but it still had meat on it.

What kind of bone? I don't know. It was quite big. Big enough to be a human bone – an arm, or something – but of course it must've been a goat. Or a cow. Deer? I mean . . .

Anyway. Moving rapidly on . . .

What did we ask her? Well, you can be sure I wasn't going to open my mouth till I'd heard what everyone else said. I'd already learned my lesson, thank you very much. I wasn't going to be shown up again. Made to look like a complete fool. I mean, honestly . . . So she just sat there like some lunatic agony aunt while everybody asked her about a load of personal stuff. Completely insane. Like she was some kind of oracle or something. Most of the time I couldn't make head nor tail of her answers. Take that first night. Carol went first, of course. Turned out she was seeing some bloke who lived on the other side of the country – in Lancaster, I think – and he wouldn't move to Hartlepool for her. (Like, no shit!!) So she'd dumped him, but couldn't get him out of her head, and now she's lonely. So she asks Babs whether she should take him back, or move on and find someone who's more prepared to commit.

And Babs says something like: 'Does a snake in the desert gather up shed skins? Perhaps the skin you have just shed was a fine one, but there is no point in looking back at it. That skin is dry now, and dead. And you are growing new skin. It is a young skin, and thin, and does not yet protect flesh beneath. Which catches on corners sometimes and bleeds. But this new skin will grow, and will better fit a body which has shifted and changed. Learn to tend your new skin. Watch each day to see how it is becoming.'

Okaaaay . . . So then Lisa pipes up. 'Baba,' she says, in that sweet and sickly Russian-tinted little voice of hers. 'What is my path, and where is it leading me now?'

'Your path is the road you are walking down,' Babs intones. 'Learn to walk it well, and it will lead you to the place where you need to go.' Well, honestly. Ask a silly question and you'll get a silly answer. At least that one made me smile. It certainly put that stuck-up little princess in her place.

Debbie – or was it Dora – has a question about her dreams. Seems she keeps having this recurrent dream of getting trapped in a cave with a fire-breathing dragon, and wants to know what it means. I think she's been watching too much *Game of Thrones* myself, but Baba, wouldn't you know it, has other ideas. 'Dream is itself a cave,' she says: 'cave in which the soul of you is stored. Dragon hoards treasure; guards it well against thieves. Sometimes, dragon guards too well. Hides soul-treasure from rightful owner. Look to the guardian of your threshold. What is hidden treasure, and what is it which will not let you pass?' Well, old Debbie-Dora lights up like a light bulb has gone on inside her head, but it didn't sound much like proper dream analysis to me. And I've read Freud, so I should know.

Dora – or was it Debbie – wants to know how she's ever going to finish some novel or other she's writing. She's halfway through it, she says, and she's been working really hard and it's all going really well. But increasingly she finds herself unable to settle down to work. She finds all kinds of distractions – 'Like constantly sharpening her pencils,' Tweedledum says, and they both giggle like teenagers – and now she's frightened she'll never get it done.

'Well,' Babs declares, folding her arms across her latest blue-flocked music-hall frock, 'it is like this. Here there is a hungry lion, prowling the jungle, searching for big meal to fill the emptiness inside him. There, there is tiny lamb, wanting nothing more than to lie in the warmth of the sun while her growing happens. Then lion sees lamb. Will he eat her? He might. And so lamb runs away and all the energy she should be using for growing is consumed by flight. So find a place lion cannot reach, and let the lamb lie down again in the sun. Lion will leave lamb alone and look elsewhere for its meal. And lamb will do her growing in peace. One day the two may meet again. But the lion will be sated and the lamb will now be fully grown.'

Er – yeah, right. So there's this lion, and there's this lamb – and then what happens, exactly, Babs? Could you maybe . . . unpick . . . that a little for those of us who actually speak English? Sheesh. Then, inevitably, she turns to me.

'Well, Beryl,' she says, 'and what would you like to ask the Baba tonight?'

Truth is, I didn't want to ask the bloody Baba anything, but I supposed I'd better show willing. And then, all of a sudden, it came to me. Well, I tried not to snigger, but I couldn't wait to see the expression on her face when I said to her, 'O Baba,' I says, 'please can you tell me this: what is the sound of one hand clapping?'

Well, Lisa looks like her eyes are going to pop out of her head and Carol from Hartlepool positively gasps, but Babs just waves one hand swiftly through the air and then softly lays it to rest on the table. Of course, there was no sound at all. And then she looks at me, and says, 'Did you hear that, child?' (Child? And I'm like fifty next month! The cheek of it!) 'That,' she says, 'was the sound of one hand clapping. When you do not understand somesing, when you are out of your depth and wish to look wise, make the sound of one hand clapping. And then turn up volume in your ears.'

I mean, what was that all about? I don't think she even knew I was taking the piss.

Yeah, it's funny how I remember it all, though, isn't it? Even though I was determined not to listen. It was all a load of bollocks, of course, but something about the way she spoke – well, it was as if the words lodged themselves inside you, whether you wanted them to or not. Like she'd shot an arrow right into your heart, and you couldn't shake it loose again. Yeah, like elfshot. That's it. As if you'd been elfshot. And to tell you the honest truth, like elfshot, sometimes it left a bit of a lingering ache.

We didn't get to the proper stuff till Wednesday. Just as well we did, because I was on the point of really freaking out by then. The whole thing was messing with my process. We were all going home on Friday morning, and I hadn't learned a thing.

Skindancing, she called it. 'I'm going to teach you to *skindance*,' she says, when we've finished our breakfasts and are clearing away the dishes into that man-sized ceramic sink.

'Thank Goddess for that,' I whisper to Deirdre. 'We're finally going to connect with our power animals.'

'Sure, I don't think that's quite what she has in mind,'

Deirdre says. 'I think it's more about . . . shapeshifting . . . ?' But what did she know? She hadn't even done her 'Introduction to Shamanism' course yet. Didn't know how to journey, or anything. Besides, shapeshifting's just another term for connecting with your power animal. Everyone knows that. You'd think Deirdre believed she was actually going to turn us into animals, or something ridiculous like that! Yeah, she was definitely away with the fairies, that one.

'So,' Babs says. 'I will meet with you all one by one, and we will speak of the animal who has found nest in your heart. And then' – she looks right at me and bares those big old pointy teeth again – 'we will see what we will see.'

Well, that seemed like a strange way of doing things, but then everything in this madhouse was strange. She wasn't much of a one for teaching in circle, that's for sure. And I could have told her a few things about how to hold a space. But anyway, we were all sent off to wait outside – polishing the mortar and sodding pestle again – until, one at a time, she called us into the kitchen. I was last, of course; wasn't *that* a big surprise. I did find myself wondering what had happened to the others, though; no one came out of the front door again once they went in. And it was the only door there was.

But I had myself to worry about now, and you can be absolutely sure that I was worried. This place was really beginning to get to me. Sometimes, I was seriously spooked. Well, because . . . well, I don't know. It just wasn't . . . *natural*, was it? Does any of this sound *natural* to you? Well, then. Anyway. She gestures at me to sit down like she's the Queen of sodding

Sheba – and then she settles back into her throne and just looks at me. Yeah! That's all. Stares right at me, for the best part of five minutes. Well, I didn't know where to put myself. After two minutes – which seems like two hours – I open my mouth to ask what the hell is going on, but she lifts up her hand and the weird thing is, it's as if she snatches away my voice. Nothing comes out. I close my mouth again; what else can I do? I think of getting up and storming out, but if this is what it takes to FINALLY connect with my power animal, I'd better just grit my teeth and sit tight.

Three minutes more. And then, very slowly, she begins to smile.

I feel the smile in my feet first, as my heels begin to hoove. My eyes slip sideways of their own accord, and all of a sudden I topple forward, landing heavy on all fours, horizontal-ed and belly-downed in the forest.

My skin prickles as if every flea in the taiga has taken up residence in my fur. Birch bark fondles me; I rub and rub till finally my itch eases. I rip roots, lick lichen, spice the forest floor with scented feet. Wild-walk and oh, I am grass-smart now; soon I'm berry-gorged and herb-full. A stream sings sunwise for my water-wallowing. I'm slink-spined, nut-nosed. I lead the world a merry dance; I'm faster than the speed of light. I'm light. I'm free. I'm free of me. I'm cud-coddled; I'm all ears; I hear how everything speaks at once.

Then ears prick, twig cracks – body shrieks *beware*! I brown-blend, change cheek. Fix on form.

Wolf.

Grey.

Heart hollers. Turntail. Run.

Trees taunt me, water warns me, birds bet on me. Wolf gains on me. Hot-haunched, broken-breathed, out-flanked for sure.

Wolf bears down on me, runs alongside me. Red mouth slavers at me, yellow eyes laugh at me. Cuts right ahead of me, snaps at the feet of me. Fall on my flank; I'm done. Then I'm un-done, un-deered. Teeth bare at me, growl grips at me. I'm unhinged, unhooved, unhinded. I'm refashioned, retongued; I open my mouth and scream.

Next thing I know, I've landed back on the kitchen floor with a thump. And Babs is standing over me, ranting at me in fucking Russian as if it's all my fault I nearly got ate by a wolf.

You know, when I look back on it all now, there was a gleam in that wolf's eye that I swear reminded me of Carol from Hartlepool.

So anyway: that was the end of that. I gibbered for the best part of an hour. Then I took to my bed, and I didn't come out again except to pee till it was time for us all to pile back into Igor's minibus on the Friday morning. Deirdre was nice, though; she didn't say much, but she brought me cups of tea and the odd plate of food. I didn't know what had happened to the rest of them, and I didn't want to know. But they all seemed happy enough when it was time to leave. Milling around Babs adoringly, sucking up to her as if she'd given them the crown jewels. Well, I didn't. I didn't say a word to her. What was really irritating is that she didn't say goodbye to me either. Completely ignored me. Well, I just sailed right out of that place with my chin up high. And I took great pleasure in throwing a quick kick at a lurking Nosferatu on my way out of that ridiculous gate.

I know. Can you believe it? You're right, I should've sued her for everything she was worth. But can you imagine a lawyer even finding her in that forest? And if one did, what do you think she'd have turned HIM into?

A shark? Hahahaha! Very funny!

I did write to *Resurgence*, though. Complained about the ad, said they really shouldn't run them any more, that it was a disgrace. Well, they wrote back to me and said they'd never run an ad like that before, not ever. They'd never heard of a bone house, or a woman called the Bąba with a speciality in shapeshifting. And sure enough, when I flicked through the old issues I'd stuck on the shelf for safekeeping, I couldn't find it either. It just gets weirder and weirder.

Well, yes, I would've contacted the others, but when I suggested exchanging email addresses on the way back to the airport, no one bothered to reply. Typical. I'd try to track Deirdre down, but it's not like there probably wouldn't be a few other Deirdres in Sligo. And I never did learn anyone's surname.

So anyway, bugger it. I've had quite enough of shamanism, thank you very much. Baba-the-sodding-Yaga there put me off it for life. I'm doing a Priestess of Avalon training in Glastonbury instead. Seems like it's going to be a lot more authentic, anyway. It's run by this woman who's a yogi as well. She was ordained by a direct disciple of the Yogi Krishknuckle, or some such person. She's very spiritual. She was one of the most spiritually influential people of 2018, according to an article I read at the Pagan Portal on Pantheos. It's really helping me to manifest my vision. Except I don't really have one yet. I'm sure I will soon.

Well, it's been lovely talking to you. We must do this again sometime. Are you going to Matthew's Lakota sweat lodge ceremony on Saturday night? Matthew – you know the one. Struts up and down the high street in a tweed hat and a frock coat. Big grey beard. Looks like Gandalf but fancies himself as a bit of an Aragorn. Yes, that's him.

Great. May we all be blessed there with the presence of the Great Spirit!

See you there. Bye now.

Namaste.

THE
WATER-HORSE

IT WAS NEVER going to end well for that girl. Not according to the customs of the day. I don't mean that in an unkind way – not at all. I knew what it was to be different, like her. Knew what it was to be a dreamer. And that girl was a dreamer. She wanted too much, but she didn't even know how much she wanted. Not till she found what it was that she wanted, and then there was only one thing for her to do.

I could see it coming. Of course I could. I was the district nurse; it was my job to know. There was no one else here with responsibility; no one to keep an eye on things, to look out for people. We were far too remote a village for that. And I understood that girl, as no one else could. I might be old now, getting on for ancient, with a body that is slowly failing – but once I was young and pretty, like her. My heart burning so brightly in my chest I could have scorched cities with it; my yearning so vast and deep it could have bottomed out the world.

So make yourself comfortable, young man, and I'll tell you what really happened to that girl whose story you're so intent on digging up. It has never been fully told before, for I am the only one who knows the truth of it. I'll tell you how it began, and I'll tell you how it ended. I'll need to remind you how things were here, back in the day. Sixty years ago, or thereabouts. Life was different then; people were different. The world was different. And maybe I'll slip in another tale or two for your archives, along the way. Because the stories of this island are like the land itself: the interlocking textures of the Llewissian gneiss that bears us now, melted and banded, and all folded in on itself. Metamorphic rock, that's what this island is made of. Born out of the most intense heat and pressure. How could our stories not be metamorphic too?

It was the books that first gave that girl away. I saw what she took out of the rickety old library van each month; we two were always the first to make our way down to it. Hastening down the road from our opposite ends of the township. She lived in the last house down the track that ended at the western headland; I lived in the last house that ended at the southside beach. We both lived on the edges, and converged there uncomfortably in the heart of things. We would meet at its squeaky side doors before Iain the driver had finished opening up the van, and she would nod shyly to me and then look away. I watched her, as she browsed the surprisingly rich selection on the shelves; I was curious about her. Teenage girls in our part of the world did not usually get so excited by books. I saw the books she took out, and I heard her when she asked the librarian to bring her more by this author or that. Yes, it was the books that first gave her away. Folk tales, love stories, poetry. Fairy tales, most of all. Andersen, Grimm, Perrault – she didn't care; she read them all, old and new. You would know all about them, I suppose, a folklore collector like you. Oh, you don't really do fairy tales? Well, not many men do. Maybe that's wise. Some of us do them whether we choose it or not. *They* choose *us*; they happen to us. They know their prey. The dreamers.

But there was never going to be a handsome prince for that girl. This island didn't do princes, and this township didn't do handsome. It is hard to imagine that it ever did.

She was the girl her family sent to the shielings that summer. Yes, they still packed up and went to the summer grazings on the island then. We kept the old traditions going, here. Longer than they did on the mainland. They used to spend the best part of three months out there, but in that girl's day it was usually only six weeks. Because of the schools, you see. The children had to go back to school. Oh, it was a fine and joyous time – like going on your holidays, you know? Though none of us had the money to go on holidays back then. So that was our holiday, our time of freedom. There was something about being out together there, right out in the hills. We didn't have much in the way of civilisation to escape from back then – no more than we do now – but we felt that we were escaping from it all the same. Freedom from the grind of crofting life, from the stifling intimacy of a tiny township in which all the houses were visible to all the others.

We were a small group who went to the shielings; mostly women and giggling children, escaping for a while from the tight-lipped oversight of the men. Well, the occasional old man came with us who had no other need to stay in his winter house. The others would only come down from time to time – when there was physical work to do, like mending a roof. And the animals came, of course – it was all about the animals. We took cows, mostly, though in later years some of them brought sheep. The good land on the crofts had to be kept vacant to grow the crops. To make the hay, and grow the turnips. To regrow the grass to sustain the animals through the winter. So that is why we all went. The animals had to go to the *geàrraidh* – the summer pastures – and we went with them. To mind them, of course.

We went as our ancestors had gone before us, for these grazing places were passed down through the generations, and our attachment to them was strong. A fine wee procession we made, walking along the main road before crossing the river, picking our way through the wet, low bog and on up into the hills – following the old stone cairns which marked the safest path. The men would come with us on the day we went, to help carry supplies. We carried our clothes and utensils in backpacks, and the dogs ran alongside us, barking as if they were happy to be going on their holidays too. *An Iomaich*, we called it – the Flitting.

Not everyone stayed for the whole summer. The older women and children went back down after a few days, and only a handful of girls were left in the huts. They had charge of fifty or sixty head of cattle, and the same of sheep, for about six weeks. Once a week, people would come out from their villages to fetch back the cheese and butter the girls had made, and to bring out anything they may need for use during the following week. There would be stories and songs during those gatherings: the summer ceilidhs, we'd call them. The young men of the village would sometimes walk up too, and keep them informed about the local news. Many a romance has its beginnings up in the hills, and a good few old married couples look back on memories of shieling courtships. Do you know that old love song about the shielings? Kenneth McKellar recorded it, back in the day. Come closer, and I'll sing it to you, though my voice isn't exactly what it once was. I'll sing you the English version, since you don't seem to speak the Gaelic.

Last night by the shieling was Mairi, my beloved,
Out on the hillside by the shieling, my Mairi, my beloved.
Mo Mhairi, mo leannan, mo Mhairi my beloved.
On the hillside by the shieling, my Mairi, my beloved.

Like the white lily floating in the peat hag's dark waters,
Pure and white as the lily in the peat hag's dark waters.
Mo Mhairi, mo leannan, mo Mhairi my beloved.
Like the lily white, floating in the peat hag's dark waters.

Like the blue gentian blooming wet wi' dew in the sunshine
are the eyes of my Mairi, purple blue in the sunshine,
Mo Mhairi, mo leannan, mo Mhairi my beloved.
Lily white, pure, gentian eyed is my Mairi, my beloved.

Aye, it's a fine old song, right enough; we all sang it, when we were together there, in the hills.

Well, the girls had a great time in the huts, playing house, and papering the walls with illustrations from newspapers and magazines. They usually liked to stay together, but that girl stayed in her family's *àirigh* alone. None of them came up with her; her brother had gone off to the mainland for work, and her mother was ill as usual. Her grandparents were long dead, and her father had died too, the winter before. *An Àirigh Fad Às* – the Faraway Shieling – that was the name of her place; it was right on the edge of our pastures. Yes, it had a name, as they all did. Names mattered in those days. Everything had a name, for everything was known to us. Every lochan, every mound, all the big rocks. They tied us to the land, and to the people that had gone before us. We knew the land, then; knew its creatures. Its stories and its mysteries. Knew the names of things. And we navigated by those names, all summer long. As children, we could tell our parents exactly where we were going or where we had been. In which loch we had seen the big brown trout leaping; on which hill we had gathered long rushes for the plaiting. We knew that land by heart; we would never get lost there. But there were cautionary tales aplenty about the bog, too. We knew the places to avoid – the places where you'd be sucked down to the centre of the earth and never seen again. Or so our elders told us. To keep us away from the quaking bogs, above all. But that girl haunted those places. I watched her, crawling as close as she could to their waterlogged edges, that threshold place where dull moor-grass gave way to a trickster's emerald green. As close as she could, without sinking.

That girl loved the moor; she was made for it. It was in her blood. She loved the wildness; she loved the freedom. Loved the solitude, too, for that was a rare thing in a crofting community in those days. She had always liked her own company; found it easier than the noisy gossip of girls her age and the bullish boasting of the village boys. Boys they were, and oh, did she not long for a man. She was seventeen years old, and she knew what was ahead of her, all right. Marriage to a man who didn't know how to navigate the soft maps of a woman's body, to excavate the deep caves of a woman's heart. A baby each year, till the black crows in their black-hearted churches frowned at their excess, and they started to sleep in different beds. Winter days spent navigating mud and dung to feed hay to the shivering animals, hands red-raw from liming the lazybeds. Cancer growing slowly from exposure to the sheep-dip. There would be no job for her – no escape that way; we were too far away from the big town, from Stornoway. And besides, she was the only one left to work the family croft. And to look after her ailing mother. She'd have no time for reading, not that girl. No time for dreaming. Not any more.

Yes, she would end up like her mother, she knew. She'd watched her, stony-faced at her husband's funeral. Women like that were not supposed to cry. Though the girl had heard her crying anyway, in the quiet of night when he'd fallen asleep in the peat-stained sheets of the bed she'd made. But mostly she soldiered on. Two children she had birthed, and the one they cut out of her womb on the fifth anniversary of their marriage. Hard enough already, her husband hardened then. The Word of God was the only word spoken in that house on a Sunday, when she would brush off his black suit for church, polish his black shoes. Soon the Bible displaced their wedding photograph on the mantelpiece, and while he was turning to God, she turned to the fields. She managed the crows on the croft just as she managed the crow in her house. She milked the cow for crowdie and fed the weaners to fatten them; she pulled dead babies out of eye-rolling ewes in the lambing snows of May.

Women like that were not supposed to read poetry; women like that were not supposed to believe in mermaids. And daughters like that girl might sometimes look longingly out to sea . . . but they stayed.

So anyway – that girl was sent to the shieling with the cows. Fine cows they were, too: the very best pedigree Highland cattle. Shiny brown coats and sweeping, pointed white horns. You wouldn't want to mess with them while they were nursing a calf, but the rest of the time they were quiet. They liked a bit of human company from time to time, and they liked her well enough. I heard her singing to them in the fields. The old laments, about lovers stolen away by famine and by war.

Yes, that family's shieling was in a beautiful spot. The old stone *àirigh* had been replaced by then, of course; hers was a new timber structure, coated with bitumen, with a tin roof. It was simply furnished, as they all were, with a box bed and a covered mattress of heather and straw. There was a rickety wooden table with the paint peeling off, and a couple of plain chairs; there was a fire at one end and recesses in the walls for storage. She was happy to be there, at first.

It was beautiful all right, but strange stories were told about those hidden glens. Strange stories about the shielings. Did you hear the story yet of *An Àirigh na h'Aon Oidhche* – the one-night shieling – way up there on the hill slopes beyond Mealasbhal? I remember my Uncle Roddy telling me about it. It was a good couple of miles away from our pastures, but close enough that hearing the story would always make us shiver with fright. Something happened there on the very first night it was built, and since then everyone has shunned it. The ruin stands there to this day, exactly the same as it was when the bravest of us went there. Just around the corner is a cliff which, in high winds, is said to make loud, unexpected and frightening noises. It was a young woman from Mangurstadh who spent the first night there. Just think of it, young man – she'd have heard the stories which already abounded in that wild hill-place: stories of sheep rustling and murderous old ladies, stories of mischievous fairies. Of lochs brimming with dark beasts. Truth is, the moor itself is a great dark beast. The burns are its veins, the black buttery peat its body. Those mountains are its great, wrinkled brain. And some nights, when the mist comes down over Cracabhal, you can imagine that beast rising up right beneath you. Opening its great maw and swallowing you all the way down.

Anyway, it is likely that the girl from Mangurstadh, on her first time at the new shieling, did not have a good night. There she was all alone, in unfamiliar surroundings, at the mercy of strange winds and hearing many strange sounds. Whatever else might have happened, she must have spent a terrifying night there, and as soon as it was light enough, she left the shieling and ran all the way back home. When she got there she was in a terrible state, rambling about big black beasts, and was adamant that she would never spend another night in that haunted hut. It would seem that the truth of her story was not doubted, because to this day no one else has dared to sleep in the one-night shieling for fear that the black beast will return.

Yes, there were ghost stories aplenty, you can be sure. But the most common of the stories, the cautionary tale which was told to the girls every year before they took to the hills, was the story of the water-horse – the *each-uisge*. We all had our own *each-uisge* in those days, it seemed – one for every *geàrraidh*. Sometimes the *each-uisge* came as a Cailleach, and the visitation of that old woman foretold a death. But usually it came in the form of a handsome young man – a water-prince, wild and dangerous. Our *each-uisge* lived down at the bottom of the deep, dark loch at the far end of the glen, across from the fairy mound. And that, of course, was precisely the place that girl liked to go best.

You think you know this story, don't you? Think it's no different, really, from all the water-horse stories you've ever heard, from one end of these islands to the other. From the Butt of Ness all the way down to Barra Head. You think you know this story.

You don't.

So she went to the shielings, with her wild heart pounding at the walls of her chest like a bird who has just been caged and knows that its confinement is for life.

What was a girl like her to do? She had no sympathy from her mother. Her mother's only advice to her daughter was that she should not read poetry any more. It would make her want too many things that she couldn't have. And there is no point to that: none at all, she said to the girl. There is no point in holding on to dreams that you can never fulfil. You make your bed, her mother said, and then you lie in it.

You know how the old fairy tales go. The good girl does what her mother tells her, and then she gets her reward. But that girl did not want that bed. She wanted something different; she wanted something more. Yes, more. For sure she wanted more! What would a mainland man like you know about the yearnings of an island woman's heart? We're a fanciful folk here – fanciful and fey. What could you possibly know about our sea-longings, our hill-cravings? What could you know about the eerie half-light of midsummer nights in the glen? I knew a woman once who could not stand them, the never-ending days of an island summer. She said it drove her half mad. She was an incomer, though; the island drives them all mad, in the end. You never saw the stars, she said, for the best part of four months. And that is true enough, but there are mysteries enough on this earth without always looking to the stars. Mysteries enough in the midnight sun gleaming on Loch na Mna, or the wind carving a channel through the wild, dark waters of Loch an Eich-Uisge.

That girl had an open and tender heart; she never learned to hide it. Never learned, like the rest of us did. But this island eats tender hearts. Gobbles them down whole.

Well, she did her jobs that summer like everyone else. Followed the cattle around the moor to make sure they didn't slip into the quaking bog and drown; fetched fresh water from the burn when it was her turn. Made her share of fine crowdie and smooth, silky butter. But she did not spend much time with the others. She often went off alone, and because she was an older, hard-working girl, and known always to have been a bit of a dreamer, no one thought anything of it. Well then, before we all knew it, the summer was gone. As the second weekend in August approached, we were all preparing to go up to the shielings to start the long process of closing them down for the season, and to bring the girls back home.

But before we could set off on that fine, warm morning, that girl came flying down the hill to the township, face wet with weeping, long red hair whipping in tangles round her face. She was hardly able to speak a word of sense. Ran into her house, locked the door, and did not come out again till the following day. There was talk in the village of ghosts, and there was talk of monsters. There was talk of the one-night shieling, and black beasts that go bump in the night. But more than all of these, there was talk of the *each-uisge*, and the rumour of it spread through the district of Uig like wildfire.

The men went up the hill alone to fetch the other girls back down; the women, they said, were to stay secure in the township. So that was it: the last of the summer ceilidhs up on the mountain ruined. It was always a grand event, you see, the departure from the *geàrraidh*. We would all go up there together to pack up; we would spend the night singing and dancing and storytelling, and we would come back down with all the supplies the next morning. Now, though, the men were playing it safe. If the *each-uisge* was on the prowl again, as happened at least once in the memory of every generation, then any woman might find herself his prey. So up they went for the girls, right away; they planned to go back again on Monday for the rest of the supplies. Well, you couldn't work on a Sunday, you know. Not on the Lord's Day. Not even to foil the *each-uisge*. And when they went on Monday, they would take their guns. They would take their guns to Loch an Eich-Uisge, and they would see to that fellow for good.

She came to visit me, the next afternoon. That girl did. When the village was quiet and everyone sleepy from the after-effects of the Sunday roast. She told me all about it; she trusted me. Why me? Well, who else could she possibly tell? The Calvinist crows in their dark churches would offer her no succour. They would scream eternal damnation at her, they would probably exorcise her. They'd preach against her from their hardwood pulpits; they'd say she'd brought the sin upon herself. Why, the sin of attracting the attention of the *each-uisge*, I suppose. Why had he chosen that girl, and not another? What wickedness had that demon seen in her which drew him to her? No, there was no logic in it. The crows didn't need to do logic: belief was enough. Belief was everything. Belief, and fear. There was no compassion in those fine Christian men. Not then, and not ever to this day. I have never seen compassion in them. Not once. But I was priest enough for her; I was her confessor. She told me how it had gone; she told me the full story.

It had gone like this.

*

The day was fine, the first time he came to her. The sky so clear and blue that her eyes ached to look at it; so warm and wide that there seemed to be room in it for any dream to grow. She stared out across the waters of the loch, watching four-spotted chasers swallow up midges; she smiled as moss carder bees grew drunk on red clover and bog asphodel. Yes, the day was fine, all right. The slow slap of water on flat stones at the edges of the loch, the distant cry of the golden plover, the hiss of the breeze through purple moor-grass and heather.

They say that a man went fishing once, up in that loch. And as he put his hands into the water, a silver trout leapt out. The fish turned into a girl – the most beautiful woman he'd ever seen. Face like the moon and eyes like stars. And away he went after her, away. He never came back. He grew old searching for her. So tell me, then, fine young folklorist from the mainland that you are: what does longing do when it comes face to face with its own reflection in the dark, shining waters of a moorland loch? What wonders might you conjure up from the deep, if only you want them hard enough?

The day was quiet and fine, and she thought that nobody was there but her.

Which was true. Until he was there, too.

She tilted her face and took in his dark, weed-strewn hair; she knew what he was from the beginning. Stared into his strange blue-green eyes, gently touched the oddly downy skin which stretched across his thoroughbred bones. He didn't stay long that time; he didn't say a word to her. Afterwards, she marvelled to herself that she had not felt even the faintest flickering of fear.

The second time he came, he lowered himself down beside her where she sat, and laid his handsome head in her lap. She could have done it then, in exactly the way that all the old stories say. She could have left – escaped him. Everyone knew how it was to be done. Could have untied the long strings of her apron, and slid a flat stone under it in the place where her thighs had been; could have left him sound asleep there, and run.

That was not the day she ran.

Instead, she sat with him there while he slept, fingers combing his weed-tangled hair, hands stroking his silky, dark, pointed ears.

The third time he came, he laid his head on her breast, and she did not push him away. A skein of wild greylags called out to her from the sky; a silvery brown trout jumped for joy out of the dark heart of the loch. He lifted his hands to the ribbon that bound up her hair; undone, she closed her eyes, and let it all fall.

There's a story about the birth of this island, do you know it? Well then, here is another for your collection. It happens also, you see, to be the story of a *each-uisge*. There were no Western Isles in those days; there was only Stack Rock in the outer seas, and that with a fine castle upon it. That castle, it is told, was once the home of a fearful giant. Oh, a right monster he was: half man and half serpent, and the proud possessor of nine fierce heads. His favourite food was young girls. He would raid the inner isles to satisfy his appetite, carrying off nine maidens at a time – one for each of his cavernous mouths. One day, a young man who was betrothed to one of the captured maidens decided that this did not sit well with him at all. So he took himself off to a certain mountain loch in which lived a *each-uisge*. The young man knew the horse well; it seemed they were both keen on fishing. And the boy had warned the water-horse once, when the men of the village had set off with the intention of capturing him – for he was a fine strong horse, and would work for them well in the fields. It was known in those days that you could capture the *each-uisge* if only you could get a bridle on him; he would not be able, then, to take on human form. So anyway: the *each-uisge* owed this young man a favour. Well, he told the horse of his loss, and asked would he carry him across to the outer seas in search of the evil giant. The *each-uisge* agreed. So they set off together, and the horse swam around with the young man on his back until finally they found the giant. The horse assumed his fine human form, and together they managed to slay the monster and free the nine maids.

But that left them with a wee bit of a problem. How to bury so gigantic a creature, even though they'd reduced him in size by cutting off eight of his nine heads? Well, he was too big to sink, so in the end they left him floating there in the outer sea, and the young man and his betrothed swam back to Skye on the *each-uisge*'s back. As time passed, the sea claimed the monster for its own. Seabirds flew in and pecked at him; fishes swam in and nibbled at him. Strong winds and waves crashed at him, scrubbing and rubbing till all that remained were the bare bones, and these turned eventually to rocks and hills and cliffs. The Butt of Lewis was born from his one remaining head, and the soles of his feet are now the cliffs of South Bernera. The eight disassembled heads became the outer islands. And that, so they say, is how the Western Isles came to be.

But my point is this: it was a *each-uisge* who helped to save the day; a *each-uisge* who helped give birth to these islands. It stood in stark contrast to the other tales – the ones which say that they're liars, and always evil. That girl knew the story, of course. And in it she found the local hero she had been looking for all her life.

On the day she ran, he had asked her to marry him. To come with him, down through the deep dark waters of the loch; down through the deep, dark waters of the world. To come with him to another world. He could change her, he said; he could transform her into a creature just like him. She would live with him forever in the land beneath the waters – but sometimes, if she chose, she could walk these hills again as a beautiful young woman. Just as he did now, as a handsome young man.

It was the choice of her life, and the only real choice she would ever have. That girl knew it, for sure. Can't you see that now, young man? But faced with a choice she had never really expected, that girl simply did not know what to do. Who knows how it is, the land beneath the waters? Who knows what it is, to live the life of a *each-uisge*? Would she remember who she once had been, or would it all fade away when she changed? How could she choose a thing when she did not really know what it was that she was choosing? Yes, she had wanted something more – she had prayed for something more. But now it came to making a real choice, she was afraid.

So she ran from him. She left him there by the lochside, his wild eyes flashing and his fine-boned arms outstretched to her, and she ran back home to the village.

In one version of this story, that girl stays home and stays safe. Marries a local lad and lives happily ever after – or so the people of this township would like to think. In a second version of this story, that girl stays home and stays safe – then dies of a broken heart. But this – this is a third version of the story. This is another story again.

What should she have done, then, that girl? Gone back to her stifling, small life? Gone back to her small life, as I did? Yes, me. I understand that girl, you see, because I was just like her. Because the same thing happened to me.

No, it was not the *each-uisge*; it was a selkie that did for me. Out of the moonlit sea he came, strong and sleek; fronds of sea fern dripping from his body onto the singing sands. Yes, when I was a young girl, something happened to me down by the sea. This sea at the edge of the world, this sea at the end of all things. This sea where the road runs out, where the heart gives out, where the spirit's lifeblood leaches out – if you let it. I haunted this shoreline as a girl. I would stand right there on those sea-battered rocks, searching for the Blessed Isles out west. When I was a child, I thought St Kilda was Hy Brasil. You know how it is – how it comes and goes, even on the clearest of days. One minute it is there, then you blink and it has vanished again. I would stand on those rocks in the face of prevailing gales and wish for magic with all my heart. Someday, I'd dream, a boat would come and carry me away. The boat, of course, would be steered by a handsome prince, and he'd whisk me off to his magical island in the west.

Instead, it was a seal-man who carried me away. He surfaced slowly from the flood tide; washed up on Mealista beach. Becalmed, bewitched, I scrambled down to him; I watched with fascination as his sealskin slipped away. I stared into his wild, animal face; saw seahorse and starfish flash in his dark, round eyes. He took hold of my hand, and we swam together under a suddenness of September stars. Yes, the first stars I had seen for four long months, glistening and glittering even through the bright white fullness of the moon. He made love to me in the shallows at ebb tide; he left me when the sea deserted the land. When the tide turned tail and ran for its life, a third of the way to Mealista Island, and more.

I knew all the stories about selkies, of course; I knew that those seals could take their human form just once a month. One night each month, when the moon was bright and full. So when that full moon next shone down on the fine, white sands of Mealista, I was there waiting for him. In flood tide and ebb, and all the tides between – he came and he went through all these long, hard years. Why do you think I have stayed here, young man? A handsome woman, unmarried, alone? I have stayed in these bleakly beautiful, godforsaken edgelands for him.

If he could have made me like him, I would have taken to the sea in a flash. I would have become seal for him; I would have become selkie for him. I'd have braved the Blue Men of the Minch with him, I'd have stolen the pearls of mermaids for him. But that gift is not in a selkie's power. That is the gift of the *each-uisge*. The *each-uisge*, you see, holds the power of transformation. Not just for himself, but for others.

He was a strange creature, my selkie. When he was on land he longed for the sea; when he was in the sea he longed for the land. And is that not given to us all, to long for what we never can fully hold? Sometimes, love is like that. Sometimes, love can only exist while balancing, like angels, on the head of a silver pin.

So I fell into such a love: I fell into the arms of the sea. I fell into the sea. Do you know the old story from Harris about the fish that fell into the sea? A Tarbert fisherman caught a particularly fine herring. So fine and beautiful was the herring, and so fond did the fisherman find himself of it, that he stuck it in the breast pocket of his jacket to keep it safe and warm. It was not the cleverest idea in the world, and, well, that herring struggled. Of course it did; it was a fish out of water. It couldn't breathe. But like any animal, it wanted to survive. So it gaped and it gasped, and finally it found a way to take its oxygen from air. To bypass its gills, to open its little round mouth, and let the air find its passage through.

The herring was happy enough in its way, they say. The man loved it, and fed it; the man sang old fishing shanties to it, to lull it to sleep at bedtime. Then, one night, the man went to the pub as sometimes he did on a Saturday. But this particular Saturday happened to be his friend's birthday, and the man had a little too much to drink. Staggering home along Pier Road, he decided to go and relieve himself into the water. But just as he was unzipping his trousers, he caught his foot on a misplaced stone, and pitched himself to the ground. The herring tumbled out of his breast pocket, fell into the sea – and drowned.

So there she sat, that girl; there she sat, in the chair where you are sitting now. Word-wounded, world-wounded. 'The thing to do,' I said to her, 'is to take your life in your own hands.' This island will chew you up, if you let it. This island, and the stories they tell about how it is supposed to be. 'Make your own story,' I said to that girl. 'Make your own ending. Whatever story you choose, make it your choice – not theirs.'

They never found her body; the *each-uisge*, they say, took her after all. Drowned her or ate her, who can know? And after a fashion, they're right. He took her. But what they never could grasp then, and what they will not understand now – when finally you write that girl's story down for all to see – is that she went back to him of her own accord. She went willingly into those deep, dark waters – and she went as a *each-uisge*.

What's that, young man? There's a knocking on the door, you say? That will be him, then; I thought he might come today. The moon is full, and this winter afternoon is quickly fading to nightfall. Go on then: it's time for you to be away. I've spoken enough stories into your shiny little machine for one day. You can let him in on your way out. He will hang his sealskin on the hook behind the door, just as he always does. It is worn now, with dark and faded patches, with scars around the neck from battles he has lost and won. He will sit there in your chair, dripping and steaming in front of my bright-flamed fire, and we'll look into each other's eyes awhile, and smile.

One final thing before you go. If you want to be certain of what happened to that girl, go up to the shielings at dusk or dawn, and find your way through the quaking bog to the rocky shore of Loch an Eich-Uisge. If you are lucky and if you're quiet, you will see them there, grazing in the bright green pastures by Allt na Cailliche. You can see them there still, they say; you can see them to this very day. A great, sleek-limbed black horse, his long mane a-tangle with pond-weed and sphagnum, with flashing white teeth and his tail held high. And beside him there, his faithful mate: a prancing young mare with a coat the colour of cowberries, her shining eyes as blue as the sky on a crisp, clear winter's day.

SNOW QUEEN

THIS LAND; THIS island of white and snow. Can you follow the sparkling motes of freezing mist through Arctic air; do you see the aurora's brushstrokes on the pure, translucent canvas of our icebound cliffs? This beauty so pellucid, so serene, that your heart would shatter if you thought it might pass forever from this world. This beauty. No wonder you come seeking it. This last bastion of ice; the still point of a burning world. I have seen the icebergs weep; I have seen the dissolution of great glaciers. Snow Queen has raised them from the dead.

Snow Queen. I imagine you've heard of her. I imagine you think you know her. A bad sort, evil through and through. I thought it too. Believed the men who wrote down our stories, for didn't they always know best? Didn't they always know true? The men knew – or so they said. The men had always plenty of things to say.

Snow Queen doesn't say. Snow Queen loves silence. Loves the silence of ice, and snow.

It is Snow Queen now who knows best; it is Snow Queen who alone has held true.

Snow Queen will make an iceberg of your heart.

*

There is no path through this snow but the path we make. In this whitening-out wonderland, the path we make closes quickly behind us and is forever gone. Listen, and I'll tell you a story as we walk. Once upon a time there was a little boy and a little girl.

I came to Snow Queen's country when I was still that girl. I followed the boy here; I thought I would save him. I thought I would save him from her. I listened to sunshine, I listened to swallows. I learned little from the surly river; too much from the self-centred stories of garden flowers. I followed the loquacious crow, and slept in the bed of the feisty little robber-maiden. I took the advice of a wood-pigeon; I rode on the back of an affable reindeer. I ate the fish of a Lapp woman, and harkened to the wisdom of the northernmost Finn.

I came at last to Snow Queen's blue-lit palace. To its dazzling white walls of driven snow; to its doors and windows of cold and cutting winds. I found him there, willingly beguiled. Brooding over her frozen lake of puzzle-pieces; the icy fragments of her fractured Mirror of Reason. Reason now all broken in the world, and she alone capable of piecing it back together. I came to him while she was gone, for away she had gone as always she must, to grant to the wintering world her gift of necessary frost. To restrain the rank fecundity of festering lemon groves; to temper the scorching vineyards in the south. I melted the lucent ice in him with hot and muddy tears; I kissed the chaos back into clear-sighted eyes.

I thought I was saving him. How little I knew.

*

Have you ever seen a polar bear die from heatstroke? Snow Queen has. Seen ice fields soften to swampy lakes; seen ice-falls plunge to a fractured, screaming demise. She has torn the rays of moonlight from her hair; she has poured her diamond tears in smoking seas.

There are no more polar bears, now; the last one died of hyperthermia. Eyes fried like breakfast eggs; blood a-boil under burning skies.

Snow Queen will make glaciers of your arteries; she will thicken the blood in your veins to ice.

We stole away her secret, you see: the mystical words that formed for us in the silvered slithers of her glassy lake. We stole away her mysteries – the ones that would, if he solved her puzzle, she'd told him, offer him mastery over the whole world.

We were not quite ready, it seems, for mastery of the whole world. As we walked back home, hand in hand, the howling winds hushed themselves calm at our bidding. The sun leapt high into a suddenness of blue sky; erupted unseasonably through clouds now heavy with melting snow. It should have been winter still, but tree buds all around us were bursting into leaf; wildflowers were springing up in the warmth of the puddled footsteps we left behind us.

Were you there when the world burned? Did you see the footage of drought in the tropics; did you read of the desert floods? The tornadoes and the wildfires, the rending earth-quakes, the scalding volcanoes and broiling skies? Were you there when Sydney drowned, when New York sank, our many-towered mythical new land-beneath-the-waves? Did you hear the cries of snow crabs in the acid-laced oceans; did you see the last polar bear's skin blister as he died?

The Devil's ugly mirror had cracked from side to side. What we thought beautiful was broken; what we believed good was evil. Snow Queen taught us to see again; Snow Queen froze the shatterings in our hearts and made us whole.

My name was Gerda, once, and this was Kay. Come with us to Snow Queen. Together, we will save the world. Snow Queen will set the world to rights; Snow Queen will set the world to ice.

We came again, then, looking for Snow Queen; we came to her crystal-walled palace to ask for help. Over scorched mountains and across the burning taiga we walked; through eldritch new forests fashioned from horns of dead reindeer and the burned-out skeletons of brown bear. We found her sitting on the sodden remnants of the last glacier; she was weeping miniature icicles onto the soft snowy fur of the last, dead, polar bear. I saw then that she was beautiful – skin like ivory, smooth as a narwhal tusk; teeth that glistened like precious pearls.

We came to her; we sat down by her side and dried her too-warm tears. And that is when the ice in us began. Snow Queen took us by the hand; Snow Queen took us by the heart. We grew cold skin over our warm, grew hard over our soft, grew icy shell over flesh and brittling bone. We were cold at first, and it hurt; ice bites. But then we felt the fire it bestows with its lengthening touch. I was born on the waxing side of midsummer, hair the colour of midday sun and eyes the colour of cornflowers. Now, it is only my lips that are blue, and my hair is silvered like Arctic moon in the long, quiet polar night. When the men come looking for us now, I make sure to show them the whites of my eyes.

Snow Queen has remade me in her own image. Snow Queen has made me lovely in her regarding.

Come; walk alongside us to Snow Queen's palace, through the snowflakes which swirl around us like falling feathers. For we are snow angels, now; we are the clear blue fire which burns at the heart of the hardening ice. We were doomed and we were damned; we were dying till Snow Queen took us, and together we restored the ice. It is ice now that will preserve us; it is ice that will keep us whole.

We have worshipped the wrong gods. Glory to Snow Queen; even her shadow is holy. Look, do you see her? She's coming now. Do you see the corona haloing her shadow-head, blue as a ghost on the inside, red as blood at its edge? A pack of sun dogs follows her across a darkling sky; the wild hunt gallops, greening, at her command.

Come with your flaming torch, come with your burning times. Snow Queen will forge permafrost from your corpse.

Listen, do you hear her, footsteps crunching lightly on crisping ice? Are you catching a glimpse of her yet, lily-white hands reaching out to us through clouds of drifting snow? Do you hear it, the birthing song of this joy-filled, whitening land?

Ice sings; did you know? Listen: I will sing an icy Angelus for you now.

It will hurt at first, and then you will feel numb. But Snow Queen will kindle you back to life. Ice crystals will fly like sparks from your fingertips; you will dance with the aurora under glittering, wheeling stars. Snow Queen will constellate you; Snow Queen will make you whole. Howl at the moon if you must, but Snow Queen will make an ice cave of your skull.

I have always dreamed of ice. Have you dreamed it too? Is that, perhaps, why you came? Snow Queen draws you to her in your dreams; Snow Queen is gathering us all in. Together, we will refashion the world.

When the ice melted, the world burned. Snow Queen has brought the ice again. She has carved new ice cliffs and hollowed out new ice caves; she has painted the sun's pink pigment on snow-clad peaks. She has hoarded moonlight in her icy passages; she has raised up ice cathedrals with windows of blue-stained glass.

The ice is coming; the ice always comes again. The ice is coming for you all. Ice will sweep the world clean. Snow Queen will bend the light that enters your snowblind eyes; Snow Queen will teach you how to truly see.

Do you understand now, can you fathom it? Ice is the new ark. Do you know what Snow Queen has laid away in the blue-candled chambers beneath her newborn glaciers? A trove of all the treasures of the world. Bearded seals and whiskered walruses, great brown bear and Arctic fox. Eagles sleep gently there, and ravens; caribou, reindeer and moose. Frozen now, they rest there – but one day they'll return. When the world no longer burns, when sharp-sworded ice has won its battle with the splintered souls of men. Snow Queen is unravelling the world; she will ravel it again in her dreaming. The great whales will raise up songs in the deep; Sedna's fingers will grow plump again, as green-tinted flesh forms on her shrivelled bones. Shamans will come once more to comb her seaweed locks; her shivering seas will teem with shoals of silvered fish. Women will marry polar bears again, and men will marry seals. Time has no hold on ice; Snow Queen will hold it tight.

The world fails, but Snow Queen will not fail. Snow Queen will not fail the world. Snow Queen is a Trickster queen; they will not out-trick her now. Snow Queen will out-ice them, in the end.

Snow Queen is the true north; she is all that now holds true. Snow Queen will save you; Snow Queen will save the world. Snow Queen will save the world from you.

Look – do you see her? Her gauzy gown alight with snowflakes, her eyes ablaze like midnight stars? Do you see her beckoning? Do you see her beckoning to you?

Go now to Snow Queen; even her shadow is holy.

She will make an iceberg of your heart.

THE SATURDAY DIARY OF THE FAIRY MÉLUSINE

WHEN FIRST YOU saw me. There by the wellspring, pretty as a picture, the perfect fairy woman in the wood. Did you think I was a monster then? It's possible that you thought me La Belle Dame sans Merci – for my hair was long, my foot was light, and my eyes were wild; you made me a garland of *muguet* for my head.

You entered into my shadow-realm like the sun; you pierced my heart with rays of blue-eyed light. You loved me, you told me, from the moment you saw me; from the moment I saw you I was lost. A great romance, you said; one of the big loves. They'll write about us someday, you said. Sing songs about us; make poems.

What, you asked, as you held my hand in yours there, by the fountain in my golden-bowered wood. *What are you?* you said – not *who*. I see now that I should have told you the truth.

My mother never forgave us for the fact that our father loved the three of us more. Loved us one after the other, every Saturday night, while she was locked away in her bathing chamber, alone. He said it didn't matter, that we weren't quite human anyway; it was then I understood how much he'd seen.

She left him because he'd watched her bathing, not for using us as he did.

A mother's love can be a complicated thing.

When you told me first that you loved me. What did you think I was, then? People are not always as they seem. Can we ever hope to penetrate a lover's secret core? There are rooms in every heart that shouldn't be entered. Donkeyskins, sealskins, singing bones – there is a chamber in mine that is full of them. Whose headless bodies do you hide in yours?

What do you think I am now, that I was not then?

Can you honestly tell me that you love me still?

What is it, do you think, that has changed?

We bided our time after she took us away, and time bided a while for us. I was fifteen when we went for him, when we cast our spells and locked him away for good. We saw to it he'd never betray a woman again.

Or a child.

A child.

What she gave us in return:

1. Meliot, banished to an Armenian castle for all time.
2. Palatine, imprisoned in the same stronghold in which we'd put away our father.
3. And me? A serpent from the waist down, every Saturday. No man could gain entrance to me then. Did she think that an appropriate joke?

It's difficult, really, to understand her point of view.

*

That summer when we were married. The summer that seemed to last forever; the year when winter never really came. The games we played in bed through the long, hot nights; the questions by which we came to know each other's truths and lies.

What is it, you asked me, that never fails to make your heart sing?

A fire-dipped fox dancing in the heart of a winter wood, I said; and I cried.

You cupped my face in your hands and kissed me; you said I was an angel. A fallen one, I laughed, but you didn't laugh back.

This morning, when you called me a monster. What is a monster, then, to you? Don't you find my tail beautiful? Am I not beautiful, wrapped all around here in the fullness of its iridescent glory? The truth is, I love my strong tail, its layered scales green and glowing like the pulsing heart of the living earth. There is a wisdom in that tail I would not willingly forgo. Not even if I could.

Not even for you.

Is to be different always to be a monster? What do you really risk, in loving what is other? How much more might you gain?

What would you do for love, I asked you, and again you didn't answer. I don't like these word games any more, you said. All right then, I said; try this. What have you already done?

*

Saturdays. It was only ever Saturdays. Only then.

Why do we choose the men who fail us as our fathers did?

I entombed my father in a mountain. What then, if I were the monster you imagine me to be, do you think I should do to you?

Is it your God who causes you to speak to me so? Who makes you think that what I am is evil? Does He tell you I'm the serpent in your Garden? The temptress, the embodiment of sin?

Is it Him?

Sometimes I think He does not love women. Sometimes I do not think He loves us at all.

I dreamed of wooden carts and pricking pins; of witch-finder generals and dunking pools. I dreamed of crosses, of nooses, of fires. I dreamed that you were standing there, watching me burn. You would not pull me, screaming, from the flames.

This story didn't go exactly according to plan. Where's the happy ever after? Did you forget the fairy tale we were supposed to be in?

This is not the story we were supposed to be in. Where did that story go?

You crossed yourself. At me.

*

What is it anyway, to be human? Are you cleverer, finer, truer? More beautiful, more whole? Does your heart beat more soundly in your breast, do you love truth and honour more?

What are you?

I do not think you even know.

I will shatter my mirror before I go. It is hard to see yourself in another's eyes.

Last night when we lay together, your arm across my waist, our feet entwined at the bottom of the bed. I counted your grey hairs while you slept.

Was I a monster then? Is it a monster who has loved the shadow of your breath, the shadow of your shadow, the shadow now that darkens your blue eyes? Will you take a candle to me now, to reveal the monster who's sleeping by your side? Will you spill hot wax on my shoulder, will you weep when I unfold my dragon's wings and fly?

Will you risk the wrath of Venus for me, then? Will you risk the wrath of your great God? Will you come for me, anyway?

Will you come?

In my dreams, it is my mother who sets the woodpile beneath me aflame.

You didn't mind at first. Laughed at my day-long baths. Said Saturday absences only made Sundays sweeter.

Secrets are secrets for a reason. It's best to leave them be.

*

Okay then, you asked me finally, when I pressed. What can't you forgive?

It was my turn to be silent.

What do you see, now, when you look at me? The mother of your children, your benefactor? The castle I built for you; the castles I built for our sons? The cities which grew and flourished by my hand? You cherished me, and I brought richness and fertility to your lands. I brought laughter into your house and love into your bed.

Where does she go, when you look at me now? Where does she go, the woman you loved who did those things? Has someone hidden her, has someone abducted her?

She is still here. She has not gone away.

She has a tail on Saturdays, that is all.

You wonder if I have a soul. Do you?

The things I wanted to be when I grew up. A serpent wasn't at the top of my list. I could have been a fairy godmother; I could have been a fairy queen. I could have lingered by my fountain in the oakwoods; I could have been La Belle Dame sans Merci.

I could have married a man who would love me as I am.

I thought that man was you.

Listen, mother. I took your curse upon myself, inside myself. I became your curse and I have worn it with pride. I understand what you do not: the body, at the best of times, is an unstable site. We cling to fixed forms at our peril. What do you think happens when we die?

I was always drawn to the depths of my woodland well. Water was my element – I wonder what you think is yours? In the water, you have no choice but to let go.

Sometimes, I find it hard to pull myself from this bath. To come back to your world – reduce myself, limit myself. The things I could have been, if it were not for you. The things I could have done, if I had not done things for you.

You drank from my well by choice, as he drank from my mother's. It's no use being sorry now.

What's the worst thing you've ever done, I asked you, and you wouldn't meet my eyes.

If I could do it all again, is there anything I would change?

Do you know what makes me weep every time? The look on my son's face as they led him away. Call a thing a monster and you make it so. He was no monster, until your people taught him he was. Until they laughed at his boar-tusk, and made of him an *other*. They cannot forgive what is not themselves. They cannot forgive themselves. They cannot forgive.

The soft down of my grandbabies' heads. Must I leave them too?

Look, I will shed another skin for you. Another skin, if only you will take the words back. The words. If only you will take them back.

*

I have some last questions for you, now. What would you risk in the face of tyranny? When did you ever take a stand? Would you have the courage to face a dragon?

You will not quench the fire in me.

I can't stay, you know. I can't stay now. I will shed this one last skin, and I will go. Look, now – have you seen my newborn wings? See how they glow; don't you think they're beautiful, too? Am I a monster to you, still? I will open my mouth and swallow this world as I have lain for years here, swallowing my own tail. I will flash like lightning through the sky; I will rip burning stars from the heavens and rain them down on your castles.

You know I will not.

I will not look back. I will not come again, no matter how you call for me.

I will not look back.

THE MADNESS OF MIS

YOU BEGGED YOUR father not to go; were worried it might not end well. But men so love their wars. He laughed, as fathers do. As fathers do at their daughters. Laughed, and went to war. Warring is how he came to be King of the World. At least, that's what they called him: the most powerful king in Europe. And with all of the other kings behind him, it shouldn't have been hard to conquer little old Ireland.

But the men of Ireland had one thing that Dáire Donn – Brown Darragh, King of the World – didn't. They had Fionn mac Cumhaill.

When you were young you heard the stories that were told about Fionn. When you were young, and oh, you were young. Even his enemies secretly admired him. All except your father. Who hated him with an unreasonable passion. Wanted to be him – who wouldn't? Fionn had everything. A free life as a wandering warrior; success and glory in battle. The gift of wisdom from the silver-skinned Salmon of Knowledge. Nine hazel trees around the well of wisdom. Nuts from those trees; Fionn ate the nuts. Or was it the Salmon? The Salmon ate the nuts. The Fionn you knew would have eaten the wise old Salmon. He had brave companions; beautiful women. It was the beautiful women that were the final straw. The final straw for your father. Broke his back. Or was it his heart? Bad enough, he growled, to elope with the wife of Bolcán, King of France. To carry off his lovely daughter as well was excessive, even for Fionn. But to invade Ireland for revenge on Fionn was excessive, even for your father. Even for your big, brown, impetuous bear of a father.

But he was confident of his victory, your father, Dáire Donn. So he brought you with him to his Irish war. What did you really know, spoiled little princess that you were? You thought it might turn out to be an adventure after all. It was the final straw, and you were young. You turned all your thoughts to what you should wear. What jewels, what gowns. To properly reflect the status of the new King of Ireland's daughter. A princess has to be properly dressed. Jewelled, and gowned. To stand serenely on the deck of her ship and watch her father swashbuckle his way to glory. Afterwards, to preen at his coronation. You grew up safe and you grew up spoiled. Your father laughed, and went to war. Bolcán of France went with him, of course, and the kings of Greece, and Spain, and Norway. Lughman, the lord of the Saxons; three kings from the lands where the sun rises in the east. Oh, it was a fine fleet; white-sailed and strong-oared. Every ship crammed with soldiers from every corner of Europe. How could they possibly lose?

Mis, they call you; it rhymes with 'fish'. Mad Mis, mad as a fish. Do you remember now? That's you.

*

The shores of Ireland loomed ahead, and a storm loomed too. A great storm on your fine fleet. Your father should have taken it as an omen, but he laughed. Wind raged; waves towered high above your ships. Thunder so loud and lightning so bright that you all feared for your lives. Were you the only one to wonder if the gods were angry? Who heard the laughter of mermaids in the heaving green seas around Skellig Michael? No welcome there for the warships of Europe. No vessel in your fleet that was not battered by that storm. Masts snapped in two; wooden sides ripped away to expose fragile bellies. But your father stood tall and firm at the bow of his ship, and the men of Europe weathered that storm. Weathered the laughter of mermaids, drew lots for the final straw.

On you sailed, then, on to Ventry; on through the black storm's dying gasps. When you came as close as the ninth wave, a blood-red sun was falling into the sea. That was an omen, after all. But so beautiful it was – so calm. Till the warships of all Europe sailed in and filled the harbour with dread.

Dread was how it began: dread. Dread and dead and dead and dread. See how you shake your head. You remember it now, their first move. You remember those fine-fettled kings of Europe. Remember what they did to the people of Ventry. Crept into their forts and burned them alive. Kings and commoners, women and children, dogs and horses and cattle and fowl. Skin fried and peeled, flesh beneath melting like hot lard. Nothing left but singed bones.

That is what the men do. That is what they do, in their

wars. When you ask them why, they laugh. But it is Mis, they say, who is mad.

Your father underestimated Fionn. Who didn't? Fionn had friends in high places. A druid told him what would happen, and Ireland was on guard. It was Conncrithir, son of Bran, who was watchman that night in Ventry. He was woken by the music of atrocity. Splitting shields; clashing swords. Striking spears, and the cries of creatures caught in the flames. Word was sent to Fionn.

You were woken from sleep that night, too; wrenched out of the last thoughtless slumber of your childhood. Lurched upright in your warm bed of fine furs, tucked away in a safe corner of your sturdy ship. Heard the screams, smelled the burning bodies. Shouts of glee from your father's men. You rushed out onto the deck and looked landward. You have always been told war is good. War is good, your father said. But it is not good. That night, for the first time, you understood what war really was. War, and the men who waged it.

You grew up safe and you grew up spoiled. That night spoiled you, for sure.

Fionn came, and the men of Ireland fought back; they battled for seventeen days. Each day, a new tragedy. Oisín, Fionn's son, easily overpowered Bolcán of France; off that silly little man fled, into the hills. The young son of the King of Ulster, brave and true with his small band of hardly more than boys around him – slain soon after they arrived. But on they all fought, and hard. War is hard. It's hard.

He wasn't laughing now, but your father was winning his war. Till Fionn called in the fairies. In they swept, the gleaming warriors of the Tuatha Dé Danann; before you knew it, the battle was lost. She was the key to it, their great, shining raven queen. The beautiful, terrifying Morrígan. Wings stretched impossibly across the sky like a vicious black storm. Her two mad sisters harried and shrieked; panic and terror followed wherever they flew. No omens now; Death was right in front of them. They had not known that such creatures existed. Scoffed at the stories of Irish fairies, and the music-filled, glittering halls they were said to inhabit in the hollow hills. 'Tales for children,' they'd said, and laughed. Never for a moment believed they were real. Laughed, and went to war. But they did not laugh when your brother was killed, or the Amazon Ógarmach, daughter of the King of Greece. They did not laugh when the inevitable happened. When your father, frenzied and furious as he watched the battle slip away, foolishly sought out Fionn.

It was a fierce fight, they said, as they squared off. As they bared their smooth, gold-ornamented swords. It was a wondrous fight, they said; such feats of skill on both sides. Fionn, the stories said, could never be defeated; your father had never been wounded in battle. It was a fierce and skilful fight on both sides – but slowly, Fionn gained ground. Swept your father's head clean off his body. Dead and dread, dread and dead.

That was the end of the great Battle of Ventry.

Mad Mis, mad as a fish – but no fish saw what Mis saw. Will you tell the story of what you saw? You saw what you saw, and what you saw haunts you still. Haunts you still, when Storm falls on Mother Mountain, her great black clouds like the raven-goddess's wing. Death-bloated bodies, stacked in piles. Defenceless in the open field. Behind some rock, where they'd crawled to die alone. Clenched hands filled with fistfuls of grass, ripped from the ground in agony. Headless bodies and bodiless heads, swollen and blackened beyond all knowing. Severed limbs and the stench of blood; the stink of shit and spilled guts. Swords discarded, spears broken. Shields rent in two. A half-man screaming still for help. No place to hide and the sky pressing down, pressing them flat. Weight of that sky, grey and leaden. Sky sagging like a dirty grey blanket and they could not hold it off. They could not hold it up. It fell on them and they died.

Mad Mis, mad Mis. There is no glory in war; there is no honour in battle. There is only the riven, blood-soaked land, churned and poisoned by so much hate. There are only the trenches and the killing fields. Rivers choked with the stinking remains of man's unique insanity.

But it is Mis, they say, who is mad.

Listen now, and listen well, for here is the story of Mad Mis; it's been brewing for seventeen days. It begins on a boat and it ends on a beach, with a battle lost and a king dead. It begins with a body without a head.

You grew up spoiled, but you grew up safe. You never imagined this. You cry and keen and criss-cross the field; you clutch at too many final straws. Pick through all the body parts; turn over every severed head. You find his carcass, broken and bloody on the sand. You know it by his hands, by his jewelled, golden rings. By the giant knuckles laced with scars that gleam in the dawn like tangled white snakes. The King of the World has lost his head; when you find it, you lose yours. He is not laughing now. They say that you drink his blood then, but Dáire Donn has no blood left. You are licking his bruises and sucking at his wounds. Trying to clean them and trying to heal. But nothing you can do will bring back that dark, laughing head. Nothing you can do will set it back on the ragged remains of his body. Nothing will bring Dáire Donn back to life.

You cradle your father's body in your arms; you stare down the carrion crows of all Ireland. Refuse them his kidneys, his liver, his guts. Refuse them the jewel of his heart. Too many, too many; they will not let him be. You scream as they peck at the oozing hole where his head once joined his body. Cackle and screech and peck and prick and they will not let you be. They fall on you like sky; they fall on you and you die.

Mad Mis, mad Mis. Do you remember how you were born? Claw at your face, and blood runs down your soft white cheeks. Soft and spoiled and nothing safe now. Nothing ever safe again. Keen as the crows tear strips from his flesh, scream as the stench of him tears the contents out of your stomach. Throw back your head, long black hair dripping tears of clotted blood. Open your mouth and shriek, as great black birds tear the fingers from Dáire Donn's hands. Toss them to each other across his corpse, cackle at his glittering rings. Tear at your gore-covered gown. Breasts bare to the icy wind and the shock of it tears at your mind. Leave your mind there on that battlefield, along with the shreds of your gown.

Next thing you know, you are airborne. Rising up above the field, up through the stinking air. Up and up, head and arms thrown back; screech at scattering crows. Shudder as feathers burst like blades from your shoulders, convulse as arms become wings. Shudder and scream and up and away Mis flies, away into those mountains like a bird.

Away she goes, Mis. Away she goes.

Everything lost. Away.

Sliabh Mis: the mountains of Mis. It is fitting that those mountains were named for you. They saved you; they sheltered you from the storms unleashed that day. This mountain mothered you and that forest fathered you; Mad Mis is their holy child. Will you sing the songs that the mountain sang, as you roamed through the folds of her green-and-brown skirts? The deep Gregorian chant of the rocky heights, the tinkling voice of the stream-strewn lowlands. The wind section sounding through close-knit trees. Mother Mountain showed you the way. Brought you to River, whose sparkling, tumbling water washed you clean. No battle, no death, no father here. Here was only now, and now was good.

How long and beautiful were the feathers you grew for wings; how thick and glossy the fur which clothed your naked body. Oh, it was a fine madness that came upon you then. You could fly; you could run like the wind! You flew from your grief and you ran from your rage; you leapt from tree to tree. You outstripped the deer and outpaced the hares. Practised the perfection of your long claws. Strong claws, and sharp. All the better to quickly dispatch the creatures you took when you needed to eat. Sweet blood pulsing down your throat; sweet entrails smearing your face. Life was good, and death came only when it must. Death came only when something was given in return.

Eating was all you did, but *terrorised* was what they said. *Killed things, ate people.* No living thing safe.

The stories they told about you made their way into your mountains. Stories made up to frighten their children. Of dead and dread, of dread and dead: the cautionary tales of Mad Mis. But you killed no one. Ate no people. Took only what you needed to stay alive. They have to say such things, the men: can't have their women running wild. Must keep the women in their places. Dress them all up, nice and pretty. Jewels, always, and gowns. No feathers and fur for them.

There were feathers and fur aplenty for Mad Mis. For the terrifying bird-woman who haunted the green fields of Corca Dhuibhne. You could snarl, and you could bite. You scared them, all right. Kept them away from Mother Mountain; kept them away from Sister River. It wasn't killing you wanted – you'd seen enough of their filthy death. You wanted to be left alone. Had enough of their *civilisation*. Had enough of men's wars. Their voices were horrors to you; you had lost your faith in words. It was not words you trusted now, but the barking of foxes in the wood. And the harsh shriek of the slate-grey crane down by the glittering loch.

*

The king didn't like you, either. Not him. Didn't take kindly to his mountains and forests being stolen away. No more hunting and fishing for the poor king and his men. And you were glad of it. No more slaughtering and maiming for sport. Sliabh Mis was a paradise for wild things, for the people of Kerry had fled from it. But the king had lost his mountains, and the king had lost his pride. A reward for anyone who could capture Mad Mis. Land and riches for the brave man who would return you to *civilisation*. Land, and the prize of your hand in marriage. What a bargain – to marry Mad Mis! But you were the daughter of the King of the World, and once you'd been known to be beautiful. Who would come forward, then, that generous king asked, to save Mad Mis from herself?

Save you from yourself, as though you were split and not whole, holy, holier than them, *wholer* than them, than any of them. Not a one of them could save you, would save you, really wanted to save you. Mad Mis wasn't for saving. But one after another they set off into your mountains, the brave and ambitious young men of Munster. And one after another you frightened them away. Clawed at them, tore at them. You would not be taken, not you. Would not be taken alive. Saw what they did to women; remembered those fine warrior men. Saw the raping, saw the burning. Saw their dead and dread. So one by one you frightened them all away. No more dashing young men to accept the king's challenge. Their greed was no match for their fear. Mother Mountain grew quiet again. Wild things crept from their holes and caves – slept safe by the side of Mad Mis.

Then along he came, your Dubh. Along he came, your love.

You had never wanted any man. You felt no lack of human company. Wanted only the rushing air lifting you up on fine-feathered wings, wanted only the singing mountains below. *Wild woman*, they called you; *gone feral*, they said. *Mindless*, they muttered: no memory, no dreams for Mad Mis.

But you know the memories of mountains, the dreams of the drowsing land. Sister River dreams crane. Flying high along the winding thread of her; standing still in the bubbling rush of her. Nesting tight in the marshy field to the side of her. Dancing in the mountains like Mis. Brother Plain dreams horse. Wild horse, galloping across the green of him, drumming hooves deep through the heart of him. Grandmother Forest dreams fox and badger – sheltering in the dark depths of her. Dreams berries and mushrooms, feeding her roots. You've heard what the valley whispers in the night. The slow conversations between stones and crows. The tall tales that magpie tells to the old ash tree where he thinks of building a nest. This land weaves her dreaming, and Mad Mis follows her threads. The quicksilver slinking of salmon and trout; the paths made through the soft bog by red deer. This land holds them. Gathers them into her dreams as she bleeds out into theirs. She has dreamed them into being through the long ages of the world. Now, this land dreams Mis. What are you, in her dream? A fleeting visitor, for sure. But she will remember you when you are gone. She will remember Mis, the wild woman of Corca Dhuibhne.

Who fell headlong, eyes closed, arms outstretched, into the arms of this land like a lover.

If this is madness, then Mis is gladly mad.

But then he came, your love, your dove. And whether you wanted it or not, you woke up. He woke you up. It was early still, but he imagined it late. He was no proud warrior, Dubh Ruis: he was a harpist at the court of the king. The last man to chance his fate in the menacing mountains of Mis. Took up the challenge that no other now dared. The king's men mocked him, angry at his presumption. But the king, all out of options, listened and finally agreed. Gave him the gold and silver he asked for; gave him the fine gown fit for a princess. Then he sent him on his way.

Dubh Ruis, Dubh Ruis. See how the wind sings back his name? He set off with his harp and his coins; he travelled to the rough wilderness of Sliabh Mis. Beautiful was the heart of your valley, and cosy your cave at the foot of the singing mountain. Watercress grew thickly in clear-running springs; the woods were lush and deep. No humans tore down trees. No foxes trapped here, no wise old salmon punctured for sport. No trace of war, no whiff of men, no stain of *civilisation*. Then one day Dubh Ruis, son of Ragnall, came calling. Love crept over the threshold of your world.

You had forgotten the music of men as you had forgotten their words. Cared only for the consonance of streams chasing each other down the mountain; for the canticles of birds playing hide-and-seek in the trees. But this transgressive melody snaked its way into your woods. It parted the trees for you and beckoned you on. Blindly, you followed its enticing strains. At the music's end you found a harp. Attached to the harp you found a man. A young, soft and handsome man. Naked, he sat on a plain brown cloak, surrounded by silver and gold. The beauty of him. The peace.

But you had never wanted any man, and you wanted no man now. Men were dread and dead; it was music that reeled you in. It ambushed you, it wounded you – as no fine warrior of Munster ever could. Music drowned out the songs of the mountain; shattered the clear-sounding bell of the river as if it were so much glass. You shuddered; young alders rustled their alarm. By the tension in his pale, strong body, you saw that he knew you were there. The music broke you open. Broke open your mouth; a groan spilled out. No words then for the wild woman; you had spoken no words for years. Words were lost in the woods long ago, for words obscure the wild. And what are words to him now, little man, face to face with claws of Mad Mis? On he played, though; on he played. As if you weren't even there. And then he stopped, and opened his mouth. Softly, he began to sing.

It was words that dealt the final blow; words that were the final straw. It was words that brought it back to you. Screams and swords, and your father's body adrift on a sea of blood. There were things that you remembered. Heads; bodies to remember. You threw your arms up over your face. You backed away. No fierce claws now for Mad Mis. You grew up soft but first you were safe. And then there was dead and dread.

The dove-man turned; he saw your body shaking through summer-leaved trees. You were flexing your wings – but before you could fly, you looked at him, and were lost. All that you were was lost, because words came back to you now. Words gathered together in your chest, crowded into the clean, empty chambers of your heart. Words made themselves known to you and you remembered who they were. Words inside undid you: they unzipped your mouth. And out they tumbled, and said. They said. The words said.

'At my father's court,' the words said, 'there were things such as that.' You nodded at his harp.

'Were there now,' said the dove-man, his speech as sweet as his song. 'Well, won't you sit down with me, and listen for a while?'

But still you did not trust these words; words obscure the wild. You shook your head; you stepped back into the wood. The dove-man turned again to his harp. You saw him watching you, out of the corner of his eye. Then you noticed them, the piles of gold and silver by his side. Words rose up in you once more like gorge. Before you could cram them back into your mouth, out the words spilled.

'At my father's court,' the words croaked, 'there were things such as that.' You pointed at his coins. Coins, and court; memories of family and home. The mountain fell away from you; the foxes receded into the wood. Blackbirds scattered among brambles, and the old crane shrieked her dismay into the midday sky. Suddenly, you found you were lonely. You yearned, now; you were ravenous. You were afraid still, but now there was something more. Something. You hungered for something. You took a step closer, licked lips that once had tasted death and tears.

'Were there, now,' said he. 'Well, won't you sit down and look at them, while I play?' You shook your head, took back your step. Put your hands to your mouth to stem the flow of words. The dove-man shifted his body round to face you. Your eyes moved from the treasure scattered on his cloak to the treasure that rose up like a flower in his lap. You stared long and you stared hard. Then you took a step closer.

'What is that?' the words said. 'At my father's court, there was nothing such as that.'

'It's a tricking staff,' he said.

'What's the trick?' – and closer again you came.

'Sit here beside me,' he said, 'and I'll do that staff's trick for you.'

Closer you came, and closer still. He could reach out his hand and touch you, if he chose. But something held you back from him. Something which knew what was at stake and knew what was in store. Knew the love he would give to you; knew the freedom that he'd take from you. An exchange you weren't sure you wanted to make. So you halted in front of him, and pushed aside the words. You closed your eyes and saw right into his heart.

And there was no harm in the gentle heart of Dubh Ruis. No harm to the fox, no harm to the blackbird or crane. No harm to Mad Mis. So you let him take your hand.

Slowly, he pulled you down beside him. 'You wouldn't be hurting me now, would you, with those claws?' Shocked at the touch of human skin – no feathers, no fur – you shook your head. He squeezed your hand; reached up and touched your face. You reached for him in turn, claws tucked carefully away so as not to tear. Examined him for wounds; found none. His head was set on his neck and his arms were attached to his shoulders and there was no death to be found in the bright young body of the harpist, Dubh Ruis.

When he entered you, the mountain screamed; when you cried out, the skies wept. And when it was over, you asked for more.

Brought her to her senses, they said – but what do they know of senses? What do they know of wind stroking furry breasts, of hot sun arousing the place between naked, splayed legs? *Senses* you knew already – but it was a fine thing nevertheless, the strong, hard tricking staff of Dubh Ruis.

When you woke, you were ravenous; your new love was hungry too. He reached into his bag and brought out a piece of bread; he offered half to you. You lifted it to your nose. 'I remember this!' you said, and 'Yes,' he said, 'you do. It is bread.' So patient, your dove, your love – but all the bread in the world could not satisfy the hunger of Mis. Away from him you ran, away into the woods to hunt. You found a young stag – you would not take a hind – killed it quickly with beautiful, long claws. Thanked it for the gift of its life; hoisted it on strong shoulders and carried it back to your dove. He would not let you eat it raw; he would not let you rip and tear. He built a fire and heated stones; he placed them into an old cooking pit. He waited till the water in it boiled. Skinned the deer and cut it, and set it in the water to cook.

He sang to you while he worked; sang of love of tribe and land. For the first time in years, you wept. And as you sat by the warmth of his fire after you had eaten your fill, you promised that you would do anything he wanted. If only he would stay with you. If only he would stay.

Such things he did for you, your gentle dove. He took you to the cooking pit; he laid you down in the fragrant, warm broth. Took a handful of fat and massaged your joints and bones; he scoured and scraped and smoothed your skin. Built a bed of leaves, of moss and rushes from the forest floor; he laid the deerskin below you and his cloak over you. He made love to you again, and you slept.

You stayed in the clearing for two months. Each day he spoke to you of the world you had left behind; each day he made love to you on your bed of moss. Each day he scrubbed gently at your skin. Scraped and flayed your life away. Slowly the fur fell off you. Your feathers he plucked out, one by one. Slowly the wild woman left you. No wings now for Mad Mis. But you wanted this. You wanted him. You thought it would be enough.

On the day that you did not then know was to be your last, he cut away your claws. Then he showed you the fine gown he had carried with him. You did not want his dress – but he was right, of course, to insist. 'You will be the most beautiful woman in all Ireland,' he said. 'And besides, you cannot go naked to the court of a king.'

So you put on the dress he gave you; clothed yourself again in the robes of *civilisation*. And when he held up his small glass so that you might see the transformation he had wrought in you, the face which stared back belonged to the beautiful girl you had once been. You did not know who she was, this child.

You did not know who she might become. You knew only that Mad Mis was dead, and no one would mourn for her now.

They said that he *civilised* you, they said that he tamed you. Those are the stories that men like to tell. Those are the words that men like to say. But it wasn't *civilisation* that led you to marry Dubh Ruis. You did not marry him for his gold coins, nor the sweetness of his harp. You did not marry him for the fine deep strokes of his tricking staff. You married Dubh Ruis, son of Raghnall, because you loved him.

You went back to the world with him. You went back to the world *for* him. You played the part they required of you; the part they require of all women. You played it well – no one could say otherwise. Put on their fine, bejewelled gowns, and a torc like a golden collar round your neck. It is the way of things; you taught yourself not to care. You took the words and turned them into poems. Three fine sons you bore Dubh Ruis; grieved for the war-making men they would someday become. At last, you bore him a daughter. *Accomplished*, they said of you now, and *regal bearing*. Bearing? – you bore what you bore, and what you bore was the loss of Sliabh Mis. There is always something lost, even in the midst of the greatest joy. In gaining your love, you lost your love. But Dubh Ruis was your love now. Your dove, your lasting love.

Nothing lasts, though, in the world of men. They could not let you be. War was in their hearts and war was in their blood, and the grand warriors of the king's court had always in their hearts been at war with your Dubh. They said he'd made them look small. They were envious of his lands, and his beautiful wife. Envious of his three strong sons, and the daughter who already rivalled her mother in beauty. So they planned their revenge, and planned it well. One day, when he was out gathering the taxes for the king, they killed him.

Well, he was gone, and nothing you could do would bring him back. But they brought back his body to you – his nightingale throat slit right through. Did you weep, did you wail? Did you drink his blood and suck at his wound? Did you fly through the air like a bird?

You did not. So *civilised* were you now that, quietly, you wept. You laid out his body, and then you wrote him a poem. So *civilised* they thought it, your elegy for the well-lived life of Dubh Ruis. So *civilised* they thought you that they did not think to watch you. So *civilised* that it never occurred to them what you might do.

You'd found the very final straw. So you laughed, and went to war.

Stay? You would not stay. You would not stay in a world owned by such men. But there is one less man in that world now. You killed him in his bed, the fine warrior who had boasted of murdering your love. Slit his throat so deeply that his head fell off his neck. And then you journeyed home.

Here you are, then; here you are. Home in your mountains, home in the wild. In the only place of comfort and safety you have ever known. There is no comfort for a woman in the world of men. No comfort in their cold-hearted halls, in their hard, stone churches filled with the judgement of their hard-as-stone God. Comfort is the sound of Owl calling in a night wood. Comfort is the solid rock of Mother Mountain at your back. There is no safety for a woman in the world of men, but there is no safety now for men in the verdant, lush valleys of Mad Mis.

Sliabh Mis is safe again from men, and the deer go gentle in your woods. They will not rape your land, or mine your mountains; they will not pollute your waters. For your claws have begun to grow again, and feathers are sprouting once more across your strong, muscled shoulders. Your teeth grow sharp, and your hair grows gently grey. You dance now like the old crane does, at the edge of her midnight marsh. Who will dance with you now, Mad Mis – with the wild, grey hag of the mountain? Come dance with Mis, if you dare. For you know the path the foxes take through the woods; you know where that old crane woman lays her eggs. You have listened to the song of the blackthorn at winter solstice, and drunk from the well at the world's end. Here you are now, and here you will linger on. Forever? You have no stories about forever. *Forever* is a word which is loved by men.

Not quite forever, then. But perhaps for long enough.

Mad Mis, mad as a fish – but who's crazy now?

I SHALL GO INTO A HARE

When we go into hare-shape we say:

I shall go into a hare,

With sorrow and sigh and meickle care . . .

Isobel Gowdie, who confessed to witchcraft
at Auldearn, near Nairn, in 1662

ISOBEL TAPPED ONE foot impatiently as she watched Clarence turn a wary eye on Rob and step smartly in front of Hattie, guarding her with his body.

'Ah. Er – see here, Clarence. This really won't do, mate.' Rob threw what was clearly intended to be a winning smile in the cockerel's direction. Isobel sighed. Clarence glared. Rob paused for a moment, cleared his throat and scratched his head, dislodging a few wood shavings that had settled on his shoulders like monstrous flakes of dandruff. 'Come on, old man. Please?' Clarence was unmoved. Isobel fidgeted. 'Mixed corn,' Rob said hopefully. 'Mashed potato. Porridge. Your favourites.'

One leg lifted; long toes splayed and then slowly curled inwards. Clarence swivelled his head and looked off to one side as if quite unconcerned by the turn events had taken. Only the intense concentration reflected in the quivering of his tail feathers caused Isobel to doubt the seemingly casual pose.

'Rob, I really do think–'

'Isobel. Please. Clarence and I are having a man-to-man chat.'

Isobel rolled her eyes. Rob turned back to Clarence, who took a step forward and half-opened his beak in a curiously sinister fashion. Rob twitched.

'Ah, well now . . . Come on, Clarence. This really won't do, you know . . .'

Oh, for God's sake, Isobel thought, as she watched Rob reach out tentatively towards the nest where Hattie sat tightly, apparently quite oblivious to the spectacle that was unfolding before her. Clarence, pushed to his limit, flew into action and stabbed his beak into the back of Rob's right hand. Rob yelped. Clarence cackled and flapped his wings. Hattie pushed herself down even more firmly onto the clutch of eggs that she was determined to hatch. She had the vacant, dreamy look in her eyes that seemed to descend upon females of all species whenever they thought about babies.

Isobel saw red. She stalked over and shoved Rob to one side. Sensing victory in the forced retreat of his enemy, Clarence threw his head back and puffed himself up to utter a crow that turned rapidly into an outraged squawk as Isobel grasped him by both legs, deposited him outside, and closed the barn door behind her.

'Sorry, Hattie,' Isobel said in a hard voice. 'Those eggs are needed for a quiche. There's no time for all this broody nonsense, and, besides, it's far too early in the year.' She tightened her lips and, in one fluid movement, scooped Hattie out of the nest and began to place the eggs carefully into a dark wicker basket. She turned to leave and almost fell over Rob, who was sitting in a heap of manure-coated wood chips, clearing his throat obsessively. 'Oh, for God's SAKE,' she said. 'Pull yourself together, Rob. It's only a bloody chicken.'

Caught in the clutches of a restless sleep, Isobel dreamed that she went into the pantry to fetch Hattie's eggs out for breakfast. But as she looked down into the basket, she saw that each of the eggs had hatched into a perfect little replica of herself. As if each egg had contained the potential for the daughter that she'd never been able to have. Mocking the barrenness of the eggs she held inside her own body – eggs that were destined to remain unfertilised. Holding the basket tight against her belly, she turned to leave the pantry – but Rob barred the way, the slump of his shoulders perfectly complementing the bleak look of failure in his eyes.

Rob sniffed hopefully as he opened the door to the kitchen, but there was no answering aroma from the Rayburn. Ah well, he sighed to himself; looked like it was cornflakes again this morning. Didn't she know it was Easter Sunday? Surely that was worth a rasher or two. He'd happily have cooked breakfast himself, but he was fearful it might be taken as a criticism; Isobel was impossibly sensitive these days.

She sat at the table, staring out across the field to the sombre grey glitter of the sea loch. She looked tired. The weight of his own helplessness sank heavily down in Rob's chest. He took a deep breath and conjured up a cheery grin.

'Morning, love,' he boomed, rather more loudly than he'd intended.

Isobel flinched, then turned her head and managed a half-hearted smile. 'Morning.'

'Happy Easter.'

She blinked at him vaguely. 'Easter. Oh yes. I'd forgotten about Easter.'

Rob's determinedly jolly smile slipped. If they'd been able to have children she wouldn't have been able to forget. There would have been hard-boiled eggs to decorate and then bury, and egg hunts to organise; he remembered it all so vividly from his own childhood. But never mind: this year he'd taken matters into his own hands. After all, you didn't have to have children to enjoy Easter. And if nothing else, it would surely make her laugh. He broke into a soft but spirited rendition of 'Easter Bonnet' and crossed over to the huge oak dresser, from the depths of which he extracted a brightly wrapped, much beribboned parcel. He carried it carefully over to the table and placed it with a flourish in front of her. She looked at him blankly.

'For you,' he said proudly.

With limited enthusiasm but an effort at good cheer, she tore off the paper. There before her – wrapped in gold-tinted plastic, emblazoned with red bows, resplendent with pink and blue candy flowers and sporting a soft, fluffy but definitely smirking Easter bunny – sat a giant chocolate egg.

Isobel uttered a choked cry and ran from the room.

Rob stared after her with an expression of utter bewilderment on his face.

*

Isobel came to a halt in the hallway and put her head in her hands, breathing heavily. She'd done it again. Poor Rob. She knew that he was trying his best. And it wasn't that she didn't love him; she did. She always had. From the moment that she'd first seen him, at that post-exam party she'd gate-crashed, back when they were at uni in Edinburgh. She'd just that week smashed her way out of an impossible relationship; she was feeling decidedly unmoored and probably slightly unhinged. He'd caught her attention right away: a much-needed oasis of self-contained calm in a room full of loud-mouthed oafs, each one of them trying to out-shout – and out-drink – the others. Rob had a quiet voice and a gentle manner, and a kind, one-sided smile which had been balm to her fractured heart. There was no aggression in Rob. There was no great drive, either – but she had enough of that for both of them, and he'd always seemed happy enough to follow along. When, after ten years together in the city, her mother had died and Isobel had insisted on returning to her family croft up in Assynt to set up a freelance graphic design business, he'd thrown himself into the adventure wholeheartedly, just as he always did. He'd learned about sheep and lambing; he'd learned how to mend stock fences. He'd given up a perfectly good career as a corporate lawyer and now worked part time at the shabby old solicitor's in town.

And in return for his good-natured support, she was acting like a prize bitch. She didn't mean to; it just happened. She couldn't seem to control her emotions any more; the slightest thing set her off. But it was hard to explain to him – to anyone, really – the all-encompassing intensity of her longing for a child. It was like a physical pain inside her chest; a constant craving so fierce that she didn't know how she'd survive it. She couldn't seem to think about anything else. She knew Rob was trying really hard to make things work, but whatever he did he always seemed to hit precisely the wrong note. And meanwhile, all around her, hens were going broody, lambs were spilling out of sheep – even the barn cat had produced a clutch of kittens the other day. Pregnant women were everywhere, too. Soon-to-be mothers in the supermarket flaunted their swelling bellies, and she followed them down the baby aisle like a stalker, sneaking longing looks at nursing pads and packs of disposable nappies.

Slowly, wearily, she climbed the stairs and stood on the landing, gazing out of the small sash window at the gloomy slate-grey loch. She sighed. She'd have a bath; that usually quietened down her fretting for a while. By the side of the bathroom door, her great-grandmother Isobel stared down at her from a grubby but atmospheric old painting. There'd been an Isobel in every generation for as far back as anyone could trace, so her mother (also called Isobel) had told her, going back to the eighteenth century, at least. In the portrait, great-granny Isobel was cradling a large golden hare in her arms – a hare with peculiarly glowing sky-blue eyes. She'd always been curious about the hare, and years ago had discovered that hares with light gold coats and blue eyes did actually exist – but only on an island off the coast of Northern Ireland, not here. Artistic license, no doubt; maybe the painter had been a homesick Irishman. She stared back thoughtfully at the woman in the portrait – a woman who looked very much like she might look, too, in a couple of decades' time, with the palest of skin and fading red hair that was liberally streaked with grey. Great-granny Isobel had a slightly amused glint in her greenish-brown eyes, but her mouth remained straight and firm. She looked as if she knew something you didn't, and as if she was very pleased with herself as a result. Isobel had always found it a particularly irritating expression.

When she was a child, she'd listened in fascinated awe to all the old family stories claiming that her great-grandmother Isobel was a witch. Not only did she have a pet hare, but she could turn herself into one, they'd said; she made the transformation simply by chanting her intention. And then she'd be seen at night, she and her pet hare, cavorting with other hares down by the loch – distinguishable from the common-or-garden creatures by the pale gold of their coats and the bright blue of their eyes. Witch or not, her great-granny was a notable wise-woman; she used to have the cure for infertility, it was said – thanks to her magical golden hare. She'd pluck fur from the hare's back, and fashion it into a charm which a woman who wanted to conceive would wear around her neck during intercourse.

Isobel sighed. If only it could be so easy.

Isobel finally gave up trying to sleep at midnight. She slipped out of bed, shivering in the cool night air. Rob snorted and groaned as he rolled into the warm hollow she'd just vacated. She pulled her old towelling bathrobe over her flannel pyjamas, crept to the window and drew back the curtain. She caught her breath. The sky arched overhead like a tented ceiling hung in subtly varying shades of dark blue velvet, and a full moon shone silver on the surface of the water. Everything was quiet; the air was perfectly still.

Down on the shore, something moved. A flash of fur; the glitter of glassy eyes mirroring the moonlight. Isobel moved closer to the window and peered out. A surprisingly large hare with a pale golden coat sat slender and motionless on the pebbled edges of the loch, its small whiskered nose turned up to the sky and long pointed ears flat against its neck. With a sudden sharp turn of its head, the distance between them shrank into nothingness – and Isobel could have sworn that it winked.

She crept down the stairs and into the boot room, slid on her shoes and slipped her grubby waxed jacket on over her nightclothes. An owl in the wood hooted its nightly omens to an oblivious world as she stole through the door like a shadow.

Rob woke to the sound of pans crashing on the Rayburn and crept hopefully down to the kitchen. He opened the door and the smoky smell of crisply grilled bacon assaulted his nostrils. Isobel turned from the kitchen counter, auburn hair free and loose around her face, and beamed at him brightly.

'Eggs and bacon, darling?'

His jaw dropped. 'Er – yes. Eggs and bacon would be just the thing. Thank you, love. Yes.'

Hardly able to believe his luck, Rob slipped quickly into a chair at the kitchen table. He rubbed his eyes and yawned; he hadn't slept particularly well, to tell the truth. He'd woken in the middle of the night to find that Isobel had gone off on one of her midnight jaunts around the croft again, as she often did these days when she couldn't get to sleep. He'd stumbled out of bed and peered out of the window to see if he could catch sight of her, and – ridiculous, really – could have sworn he'd seen a couple of pale, golden hares playing in the moonlight by the loch. He'd gone back to bed, convinced he was still half asleep and dreaming, but for the rest of the night he'd kept waking up from oddly realistic nightmares about monsters, part human, part animal – no; actually they were sometimes one and sometimes the other – who'd clearly cast some sort of spell on Isobel, because she'd let them all move into the house and sleep in their bed. The Easter Bunny from yesterday's giant chocolate egg had played a particularly vivid role in one of the dreams, he seemed to remember. It had –

He blinked, bemused, as Isobel danced over with a steaming cup of freshly percolated coffee.

'You . . . well, I must say, you seem very cheerful this morning.'

'Yes, darling. I do, don't I?'

Rob smiled up at her helplessly. He really didn't understand Isobel; not now, and not on the day they'd met – thirteen years ago – at the party his flatmates had insisted on throwing after their final exams. She had burst into the room at midnight like a blazing red star, and he hadn't been able to take his eyes off her. She had stroked his floppy brown hair back from his forehead, gazed deeply into his black eyes, and called him 'alone and palely loitering'. At the time he'd had no idea what she meant, though he'd wondered if perhaps it had something to do with the fact that he'd been feeling a bit nauseous after one too many glasses of Tony's rum punch. It had certainly deprived him of the capacity for intelligible speech. He had been perplexed, but smitten. Even then, he suspected that he'd turn out to be a bit of a disappointment to Isobel in the long run, but when she got an idea into her head there was little short of an earthquake that could shift it. So they'd been married within six months, and everything had gone quite smoothly until they'd decided to try for a baby. He sighed. That was when it had all begun to fall apart. And no matter how hard he tried, he couldn't seem to find anything to do which might make it better. The one thing she needed – a man to fertilise her eggs – was the one thing he couldn't give her. And no matter how he tried to approach the subject, it was something she simply refused to talk about.

So he watched now, groggy, mystified, as she sailed around the kitchen and eventually placed before him an enormous platter of fried eggs, bacon, tomatoes and mushrooms. Some strange new charm she was wearing around her neck dangled for a moment over the plate – something golden but curiously furry – but then she sashayed back to the counter and popped bread into the toaster; she swayed from side to side to the jaunty rhythm of Bill Withers' 'Lovely Day', which trumpeted from the radio like a herald of good things to come. Entranced, Rob followed her with his eyes, and the forkful of food that he had been conveying to his mouth missed completely, smearing bright yellow yolk all across his jaw.

At around six o'clock Rob entered the barn, basket in hand, whistling tunelessly as he crept over to the chicken enclosure.

He didn't know where Isobel had got to, so he had thought he'd just collect the eggs and put the chickens to bed, to save her the job. Do something nice for her, in return for the very fine breakfast she'd produced that morning. As he headed for the nest boxes at the back of the barn he noticed to his surprise that the broody coop had been set up in the corner, inside a small mesh run to keep the other hens – and Clarence – out. He bent down and peeked in. Yes, there was a hen in there, and as far as he could tell in the shadowy gloom it appeared to be Hattie. He raised an eyebrow; Isobel had obviously had a change of heart. She really had been in a much better mood today – almost like her old self, in fact. He blushed to remember the afternoon's activities; he wasn't sure the antique satin eiderdown on their bed would ever fully recover. It had been a long, long time.

Rob moved in closer to check on the contents of the food and water containers inside the run, when something in the nest box caught his eye. He clambered down onto his hands and knees, and squinted into the darkness where Hattie sat, flat and still. And he blinked. Because, bulging out from under Hattie's right wing was something that looked suspiciously like a large blue egg. A seriously large blue egg. Rob closed his eyes and shook his head vigorously, but when he opened them again it was still there. And what's more, the egg – if that was what it was – appeared to be emitting a faint glow. He reached out a hand to open the run, when he felt a strange prickling at the back of his neck. He whipped his head around to look behind, unbalancing himself a little in the process. Isobel loomed over him with an odd little gleam in her eyes.

Rob let out a small shriek and then snickered in embarrassment. 'Ah . . . hello, love. You startled me.'

She smiled enigmatically.

'I . . . er . . . I just came down to collect the eggs.' He cleared his throat nervously. Not that he had anything to be nervous about. Whatever was the matter with him? 'You decided to let Hattie sit, after all?'

Isobel shrugged. 'She was so determined. It seemed a pity not to let her.'

'Well, that's wonderful. How nice for Hattie. But . . .' he trailed off uncertainly, glancing back at the nest box. 'There seems to be a rather . . . unusual . . . egg in there.'

'Nonsense, Rob. Whatever are you talking about?' The smile was wider now.

'Honestly. I caught a glimpse of it just now. It's far too big for a hen's egg. Bigger than a goose egg. It's enormous. And it's blue.'

'Blue.' Isobel rolled her eyes, and Rob felt himself blush. 'Of course it's blue. Hattie's an araucana, after all. And you know perfectly well that araucanas lay blue eggs.'

'Yes, but have you seen the size of it? And it's glowing!' Isobel laughed out loud. 'No, really, Izzie. I'll show you.' He turned back to the door of the run, but she reached out and clamped a surprisingly firm hand on his shoulder.

'Rob, darling. You're imagining things. And anyway: I think it's best if you just leave the hens to me, in future. You have quite enough to do around the croft as it is.' Firmly, she extracted the basket from his hand. 'Why don't you go back to the house and put the kettle on?'

For a moment Rob thought of persisting, but an image of this afternoon's activities flashed into his mind, followed by the memory of this morning's perfectly cooked breakfast. He closed the mouth that he had begun to open, and glanced down at his watch.

'Too late for tea. Just about time for a glass of wine before we eat, don't you think?'

Isobel produced her enigmatic little smile again. 'Oh, I don't think so. I don't think I shall be drinking alcohol again for quite a while.'

A few weeks later, looking for Isobel, Rob peered into the barn. She sat cross-legged on the floor in front of the broody coop in which Hattie still appeared to be resident. She was humming a lullaby; her hands rested on the gentle, barely perceptible swell of her own belly. Silently, hopefully, he crept away.

Being pregnant seemed to have changed Isobel, Rob reflected happily over their usual bacon and eggs, one Sunday morning around midsummer. It wasn't just the usual clichés – though she did seem to be a lot less brittle these days. Her face and eyes positively glowed, and she oozed contentment and ease. But it had changed her creatively, too. She still kept her graphic design work on the go – after all, along with his soliciting, that was what paid the bills. But she'd eased off a little, and suddenly she'd started to paint again. She hadn't done that for years. She'd set up her easel and arranged her paints in the bedroom that had always been set aside for their first child. Now the room smelled strongly of turpentine, and was cluttered with brightly coloured canvases which clashed uncharacteristically with the tastefully neutral antique white walls. Curiously, most of the paintings seemed to feature a golden, blue-eyed hare.

On the two hundred and seventieth day after Easter Sunday, early in the morning, the enormous, glowing blue egg finally hatched. Isobel watched as it cracked open, and out popped a perfectly formed leveret with bright blue eyes and a beautiful golden coat. She opened the door of the run; Hattie squawked plaintively as the baby hare ran through the barn door and out towards the loch – where an enormous hare with identical colouring sat perfectly still on the pebbled beach which fringed it. With a sudden sharp turn of its head, the distance between them shrank into nothingness – and Isobel smiled as it winked.

Isobel gasped and clutched at her belly as her waters broke, and the warm liquid seeped through the straw and down into the soft brown earth.

The baby was born late in the afternoon.

Speechless, Rob looked down at his daughter. She looked so delicate, with her peachy skin and the strangely thick pelt of golden hair that covered her scalp and dusted the tips of her large, slightly pointed ears. He reached for her tiny fist, and smiled down into a pair of glowing, sky-blue eyes.

THE WEIGHT OF A HUMAN HEART

Ibor Cind Tráchta, Ulster, Ireland

EMER: So there you are: the deceitful slut who thinks to steal my husband. Skulking behind him like the coward you are. Come out of there, Fand. Face me, if you dare.

FAND: Peace, Emer. Lay down your knife. And tell your fifty friends to do the same. Killing is not the answer to our differences.

EMER: Our differences? *Differences?* Is that the only word you can find for what you have done? You have torn apart my life, ripped out my heart. The first blood spilled between us was mine, not yours. But mine is an honest blade, at least; there is no deceit in it. Killing is what it is made for. Just like him. Killing is his profession; it's what Cú Chulainn does best. And maybe he's right, after all. Maybe killing is the only decent response to such a faithless world.

FAND: Killing me will not return him to you. Do you think you will win him back by murdering the one he loves?

EMER: The one he loves? He loves me, and always has. I am his wife. I have slept beside this man for years – I know him. As I know you for the thieving whore you are. Mark me, Fand: do not underestimate me. I'm a woman who is known for her words. For the truth of them, and their power.

FAND: Indeed. He always says you talk too much.

EMER: And now here he is. Cú Chulainn, the fearsome Hound of Ulster. Following a fairy round like a slobbering pup.

FAND: A *fairy*, Emer? You know better than that. It is said of you that you are good with words, but it is also said you are wise. There is no wisdom in these words; no wisdom in this path of knives.

EMER: Oh, I am good with words – don't doubt it. It was I who was crowned queen of all the women of Ulster by the trickster Bricriu, on the strength of my way with words. My husband there – the wretch who has just risen rumpled from your bed – chose me because I was good with words. I matched him, riddle for riddle, when first we sat down together to determine if we would wed. That was what he wanted, once: a woman who could match him in every respect. But his vanity has grown great over the years, and the words of others have no more import than the yapping of dogs snapping at his heels. You will not take my voice from me, though, for all your Otherworldly magic. I'll take yours from you: I'll slit your treacherous throat. You people of the hollow hills are full of lies and mockery. And I would have you silenced.

FAND: And yet your words are not winning him now. See how he frowns at you?

EMER: He will not stop me, though. He might betray a wife, but he will not set his hand against her. This is between you and me, now, Fand. Just between you and me. Are you too cowardly to face me, woman to woman?

FAND: I will not fight you this way, Emer: my power is

stronger than your knife. This is not about you; it is about my love for him. I have no wish to do you harm.

EMER: You have harmed me nonetheless. You have broken my life. He has taken lovers before, and still been husband to me. But this fever of love which has come over him, this spell you have cast on him . . . in leaving me for you, he has dishonoured me before all of our people.

FAND: Then maybe it is against him that you should bring your knife?

EMER: Maybe I should, Fand. But somehow, it is your lily-white throat that my blade thirsts for. Is there no honour between women? Would you break a marriage for your pleasure? Do you care nothing for another's pain?

FAND: What has been between the two of you in the past is not my concern. I love him. And he loves me. See how, even now, I am the one he stands with.

EMER: Loves you? He doesn't love you. He wants you, that is all. He is a man. So everything new to him is bright; everything familiar grows bitter. What hasn't yet been had is exalted, what is already possessed is dismissed. I was never enough for him. And you won't be, either.

He thinks he loves you best now; you're his newest love, and bright. But in the end, he will love the woman best who loved him first. Who has loved him down all the days, through all the times when love seemed lost.

FAND: Woe to her who gives her love to a man if he takes no heed of it. It is better for that woman to be cast aside if she is not loved as she loves. And Cú Chulainn might have tired of human loves – but he will not tire of me.

EMER: Oh, I'm just a mortal woman: straight up, no frills. And I know your kind. You fish for human men for sport, hooking them fast with silver-spangled dreams. And how could he ever have resisted you? You came to him first as a bird.

FAND: I came to him first as a bird, for I am as much bird as woman.

EMER: But he was a man for killing birds, did you ever think of that? Do you remember, by chance, the day the two of you met? The beautiful seabirds he killed for his mistress's pleasure? Perhaps you saw it, while circling the lake on your silky white wings? Or was that before you happened by? Then let me tell you how that story went.

We were gathered as always to celebrate the feast of Samhain on the Plain of Muirthemne; a beautiful flock of white seabirds landed on the lake nearby. His mistress – which one was it now? Eithne? Derbforgaill? – I fear I am losing track – declared her desire for a pair of those birds. In no time at all, every woman there was clamouring for birds of her own. 'One for each shoulder!' they coyly enjoined. And so he brought them all down with his sling – every last white-winged, freedom-loving angel. In doing so, he killed them, of course; the shock of it was too great for their tender bodies. So he calmly handed the dead bodies round: warm still, but hearts no longer a-flutter in their beautiful soft breasts.

At the end of it, there was no bird left for me. There's an irony there, when I think of it now. Though this, I should tell you, was no matter for regret; I've never been a woman to imprison what is made to be free. Nor understood men's penchant for killing for sport. But Cú insisted; he would have it no other way. I would have my dead beauties whether I wanted them or not. The next pair that flew by would be mine.

Well, you know the rest. Along came two white seabirds, joined by a golden chain. I begged him not to shoot at them; these were clearly no ordinary birds. But Cú is a man for the killing; he can never be held back from it once the idea has taken hold. So he took up his stones, and threw them one by one. All fell short – till finally, inevitably, one seemed to have struck home. But it had passed through the wing of one of the birds; they cried out their displeasure, and then they flew away. You were that bird, Fand; you, flying by with your sister, Lí Ban. Do you make a habit of falling in love with those who begin their courtship by trying to kill you? Is this the kind of man you want to have?

FAND: Is this the kind of man you want to keep?

EMER: He might be flawed, but he is my husband. Mine. I gave him my word. I gave my love, and my life, and he gave me his in turn. But there is more honour, it seems, in a wife's word; more fidelity in a wife's heart. I have never wanted anyone but him.

Why do I cling, you wonder, to what is so unutterably flawed? Is a promise not reason enough? Then think on the years we have spent side by side; the years that have bound us together. I have measured my days by his battles, mapped out my life by every scar on his body. I've tended and healed his wounds. I carry his stories, and he bears all of mine. There is something between a man and his wife which is greater than the two of them. A new organism – a conscious thing – that otherwise would never have been born. It will die if we are severed from each other now.

And what will I be if he leaves me? What could I ever become? I am no longer quite so young. A lonely old age awaits me, Fand, and I had not planned for it. I am too small to fill our bed alone.

FAND: And a barren bed it was, Emer. At least I might give him the child you never could.

EMER: You cut deep, Fand. Even without a blade.

FAND: I'm . . . sorry. That was beneath me.

EMER: Indeed.

FAND: And yet you choose this moment to sheath your knife?

EMER: My mind is no longer clear. Memory is a trickster book; it opens its own pages at will. And I am remembering things now . . . He had a child once; did you know? He killed him. In the end, it seems, he always does. He killed his only son. A boy just like him, as beautiful and strong as his father.

No, you are right: that child was not mine.

It all began before we were wed – in those early days when first we fell in love. My father was determined; he would not have me marry him. No good would come of it, he said – and my father was right, for in the end Cú killed him too. But I'm running ahead of myself; one killing at a time. My father sent him away, on the pretext of setting him a test. Cú must go, he declared, to Scotland, and there must apprentice himself to the mighty warrior-woman Scáthach. My father, of course, hoped that Scáthach would kill him – but that was not to be. What *was* to be was that Cú trained with Scáthach, defeated her rival Aife for her, and spared Aife's life – on the condition that she would lie with him and bear him a son. He'd already, at that point, taken Scáthach's daughter as a lover, and some say he also slept with the great teacher herself. He wasn't a man, even then, to hold himself back. Aife had no choice but to consent to her own violation, and he left her pregnant as he'd planned. And then he came home, and married me.

So it was Aife's child who came sailing one day to Ireland, for Cú had asked her to send his son to him when he turned seven. But he had also lain three *geasa* on the boy while he was still freshly minted in his mother's womb. He must not turn back once he began his journey; he must not refuse a challenge; and he must never tell anyone his name. And so it was that, when Conall Cernach asked who he was when he arrived on the shore there at Dún Dealgán, the boy could not tell him. Conall challenged him, of course, but the boy fought him and easily won. Conall was humiliated by his defeat at the hands of a child, so Cú Chulainn then approached him, and asked the same question. The child replied – listen well to this, Fand, and tell me when this story is done that your heart has not broken in two – 'I cannot tell you my name,' he said. 'But if I were not under a command which forbids me, there is no man in the world to whom I would sooner tell it than to yourself, for I love your face.'

I love your face. What did the great Hound of Ulster do then, Fand? Did he take pity on a seven-year-old child who was bound under a *geas* to tell no one his name? Did he remember the *geasa* he had placed on his own child, in his mother's womb, all those years before? He did not. Instead, he challenged him to fight. A seven-year-old boy who had effectively told him he loved him, face to face with the greatest warrior Ireland has ever known. 'Honour' he called it, and I tell you, I have grown wearier of that word than I can say. There is no *honour* in their honour; it's no more than an excuse for childish chest-beating. A pretext which permits them to ease their *ennui*. By picking a fight with anyone on whom the sun shines, while they themselves stay shackled to shade.

But I digress. I ran to Cú's side; I warned him not to fight. I told him that the boy was his; it was clear to me, who loved him. But it's not for women to meddle in men's affairs, Cú said. And even if he is my son, he said, I will kill him rather than have my countrymen dishonoured. And so he did. Fought and killed his own child.

I – oh, there is a harshness in the souls of men that makes the gods weep.

Well, he could not speak it himself, so I will say it for him. The boy's name was Connla. Connla, and his killing was a wicked and a wasteful deed. So I found myself wondering then, Fand – though I tried so hard to put it out of my mind – if my glorious hero there might someday kill our son, too. If ever we should be fortunate enough to have one. And I realised that I could not trust that he would not. That perhaps the gods were right to refuse me a child. For he would not, in such a case, take account of the grief in my heart – no more than he had listened to me when he took up arms against Connla. His warped sense of *honour* would overcome all.

I – have not spoken of these things before. I cannot think why I speak of them now, to you.

I am seeing a man who is unworthy of me.

I am seeing now, and perhaps too late, that it was at that moment that he lost me.

FAND: Yet you fight for him now, and hard.

EMER: I fight for my own pride, I think, and maybe not for love. Ah, the truth is, Fand, I am tired of it. Tired of the fighting, tired of the slaughter, tired of the killing code of the rabid-mouthed warriors of Ulster. I am so very tired of heroes, if truth be told. They do not serve life.

And he does not serve me. Look how I come here armed with a knife – how my instinct was also to kill. I have seen too much death; I have become too accustomed to it. It was only the memory of Connla that gave me pause.

I relinquish my fight as I relinquish my knife; it is true that you love him more. Take him, then. He is yours.

Come now, Fand; isn't this what you wanted?

FAND: I will tell you a story, in turn, for your words have touched something in my heart that I did not know was there. You speak of the failings of husbands; I will tell you the story of mine. His name is Manannán mac Lir: Manannán, son of the sea.

I wanted to marry the sea. I dressed myself for him in a white-frothed gown; I danced on the strand for his pleasure. And when he came to me in flood tide, the crests of his swollen waves surging up my thighs, I gave myself to him there and then.

I thought I could tame the sea. But he's as fickle as the foam on the waters over which he presides. The moment you reach out for him, he dissolves before your eyes.

It's our longings that are the undoing of us, and I longed for him each day. Through all the years I cast my shadow on him, I wanted him for my own. I flirted with him; I teased him. I swooped down and brushed the tips of his waves with my wings. He tantalised me in turn. Gave voice to the ebbing tides and had them sing me love songs. Hid messages in conch shells, wrote my name with the stones and bones he washed up on the beach.

I fell in love with the sea. Do we always yearn for the element that's not our own? Do we always hunger for something that we ourselves can never be?

It was never going to end well, and it didn't. He left me last year to return to his woman in Beara, but he did not stay with her long. It is said that she stands on the heights of Cill Chaitiairn, looking out to sea; she is waiting again for his return.

I fear that woman will be waiting a long time.

EMER: Your Otherworld, it is said, is a country filled with beauty and joy. Is there heartache, then, even in the Land of the Living?

FAND: There is sadness woven into the fabric of every world, but it is weariness, perhaps, which lies at the heart of mine. I envy you the brevity of your mortal life; the passion that makes you burn so bright.

EMER: Bright? If you sliced open this chest and tore apart the cage of bones which binds it, you would see no fire burning in my heart.

Come, look. I have put aside my knife. Your people, it is said, see deep and true. Come close now, Fand, and look into me. Fetch your rock hammer and your hand lens, and I'll show you how to dissect the landscape of a human heart.

It's a strange geology, do you see? A sack filled with stones, packed tight in the sediment of the years. Can you fathom its fault lines, discern the strata of its sorrows? Each layer holds a pebble for each hurt, a rock for each betrayal. It would take me an age to name them all, but let's see what we can find. Look: there's gneiss there, down at the bottom: the oldest rock of all. A coarse-grained stone for Scathách's daughter, another by its side for Aife. Above it, a layer of granite. A storm-coloured rock for the absence in his eyes on the day he stole me from my home – when he caused my father to falter, and plummet from the walls to his death. Twenty-four silver pebbles beside it, one for each of the men he killed that day. My father's men, who I had grown up with; men who had protected me all my life.

A layer now of limestone, fashioned from the crushed shells of what once were living things. The palest of stones – from the bones of dead molluscs – for the hundred and fifty women he slaughtered last year. They'd tormented his favourite, Derbforgaill, and causing her death was wrong. But a hundred and fifty butchered women to assuage a warrior's outrage? And look, here's a coverlet of coral-gravel – grain after grain of it, piled high like the wall of corpses he made of Mebd's bright army. So many sons fatherless because of him. So many fathers sonless because of him. So many husbands, wifeless. When will it end, the killing? And if I am bound to the killer, is their blood also on my hands? I fear that blood on my hands.

Rise a little higher now, chip away that crust, and reveal the volcano at the crest. Look – there's my blanket of lava-formed basalt, black as the Morrígan's beak. A fire-forged bauble for each of his mistresses, too many for me to name. There's only one diamond, and that's for Connla: the hardest, shiniest hurt of all. And perched there on top, a single wild sea-pearl. That one's for you, Fand; it's as pure and pale as your beautiful, merciless face. The lightest of burdens, but the final affront. The card that brought the whole house down.

So there you have it, my white-winged foe. My sack of sorrows, my burden of boulders, the weight of my human heart. What does your bird's heart make of that?

FAND: A bird's heart is no mausoleum; it does not house cairns constructed to commemorate the ever-swelling numbers of the dead. A bird's heart is built for efficiency. My heart is made to serve my wings, and my wings are served also by wind. My heart, then, Emer, is a lover of wind. I am a creature bound to ever-shifting air; it flows through my feathers and leaves no trace. I do not seek to hold the wind, and nor do I spurn the tempests it turns on me. I shape my wings to it, I accommodate its gusts; it passes through me and travels on its way. I am not defined by the weather through which I fly; it simply does not accrete.

But I will not add to the sorrows of your heavy heart: I take back my pearl. See? There, it is gone. He is yours.

EMER: I – do not think I want him. I do not think I can. I cannot live again with such a man; I have seen him now too clearly for what he is. Such sights cannot be unseen.

FAND: Emer, the hour is not too late. I have lost him anyway; do you see how his eyes now shine as he looks at you? And were I in his place, I would love you always, too; I would never waver. You came here as the finest of warriors would, fighting for the only thing you could not bear to lose. I have what I deserve, and that is nothing. I have wronged you, and hurt you deeply. And I am sorry.

EMER: And what of you, then, if I should take him now and go?

FAND: I'll leave this place – return home. I will mourn, for a while, the death of another love, then I'll take to the skies, and fly. To the Blessed Isles in the west, or the many-coloured plains of Mag Ildathach.

EMER: What are they like, then, your Otherworldly isles?

FAND: There are lands beyond the waves which few mortal eyes have seen. The sea is still there – still as glass; it offers itself as mirror to a mild but mutable sky. On Emain Ablach, island of apple trees, the air is thick with blossom and bees. On Tír na nÓg, where Niamh still mourns Oisín, the moon is always full, and stars beam blessings brightly throughout the day. We do not lack for nourishing food and drink; there is music always, and song, and dance. It is a strange place, Emer, and not to be taken for granted; the Otherworld has perils of its own. But if your heart is honest, and your words are true, the veils which obscure the sight of humans will lift for you. You will see the many-layered worlds for what they are.

EMER: My heart is heavy now for lack of wings.

FAND: Then come with me, beautiful queen, and leave your sack of stones behind. Let me bring you to the Isle of Women; we'll walk together on its shining, pearl-white shores. We'll take up strong and silvered threads, and weave our world anew. Will you come, then, Emer? Will you come? Will you let me heal your heart of the heaviness of men? The element you cleave to is earth, but its gravity pulls you down. I will teach you to cleave to air; I will show you how to grow wings. Take my hand, and I'll show you how.

Look. It is like this.

Fly, Emer; come with me into the sky. Unfurl your new-found wings, and fly.

Tír na mBan (Isle of Women)

EMER: You spoke true when you told me there is no weight in the heart of a bird, just the bright swiftness of shifting life. I have been the shadow on the upturned face of the cloud; I have tested my wings against the darkest face of a storm-strewn sea. I have eaten the silver apples of Emain Ablach; plucked ever-living flowers from the plains of Mag Mell. I've swum in the ocean at the edge of the world, and laughed my cares away in the flame-lit feast halls of Tír na nÓg.

When you turned to me and held out your hand, the long centuries you've spent on this Earth stretched out between us. Your otherness, your knowledge, the way you see everything true. How could I ever aspire to it? But there was no loftiness in your eyes, no sense of patronage in your manner. You brought me to this place as an equal, and showed me the safety of sisterhood.

I do not think much of my old life, now; I do not think much of Cú. The prophecies said he would die young; perhaps that's for the best. You say that time runs differently in this place; that if I returned to my world now, a hundred years might have passed for each year here. I wonder, sometimes, what its future holds. Perhaps we'll fly there together one day; I wonder what we would see? Will the men have stopped their fighting; will the warriors of Ulster have finally laid down their swords? Will peace settle over the island of Ériu, and all hearts be light as a bird's?

For now, though, I am content; the dancing breeze from Tír Tairngaire has swept my cares away. And I have you, my beautiful Fand, glowing always like the evening star at my side.

FAND: When I turned to you and held out my hand, you stood there, tall and proud, like the dignified queen you are – but cloaked in the darkest solitude, like a shroud. I loved you first, as he did, for the artistry of your speech; I loved you next for your geotectonic heart. Where you saw boulder, I saw bedrock; where you saw crack, I saw lush canyon. The burning core of a volcano in you; the molten power of earth. I loved you then for your honesty – an integrity which did not falter under the fathomless sorrows which weigh down a human heart.

I am no oracle; when I reach for the future, mist gathers before my eyes. But they will remember you, I think; just as they will remember your Cú. They'll sing of the only jealousy of Emer, and the fickle ways of her white-winged fairy foe. Yes, we'll fly back together one day, and see what your poets have made of us. We'll see if they told our story true.

But now, my Emer, night is falling; the shadows will soon roll in from the Plain of Two Mists. Let's go home.

FLOWER-FACE

I SEE YOU, GWYDION. I see you, tucked up tight in your house of stone. You think you're safe there, don't you? Dream on. Dream your fine dreams of magic and gold. I see your dreams, and I'll haunt them. I'm an owl now, a screecher, a creature of the night. And you're no safer from me than I was from you, back in the days when you enjoyed the fullness of your power.

Do you know I'm here, yet? Do you dream of me, Gwydion?

You will.

Do you know who I am? I'm the woman you created; the woman you imagined you owned. I'd say you thought you owned me body and soul, but *soul* wasn't part of the deal. Making a girl out of flowers was one thing, but even you couldn't cook her up a soul. Don't worry, though, little man; I conjured up a soul of my own. Made it out of flowers, too; it seems to be all the rage. But I fashioned my soul from the flowers of the night. Evening primrose, moonflower, catchfly. *Catchfly*, Gwydion – think well on that.

Pretty little Flower-Face, meek and mild; that was the woman you thought you'd made. Just the sort of woman you need, I'd say, to satisfy the hungers of powerful men. And oh, what men you were, who made me! Gwydion the crooked enchanter, and Math the flawed king: a fine pair of fathers, to be sure. But what good could ever come out of a man as deceitful as you? What good from a king who couldn't survive unless he sat with his feet in a virgin's lap? Really, my dear – you couldn't make it up. Well, you saw to it that Arianrhod wouldn't get *that* job. No more virginity for her. What a fine brother you were to her, Gwydion. What a fine young man you must have been.

I admire her, Arianrhod. Always did. She pulled herself together after you forced yourself on her; she got to do her own thing. Independent and alone in her beautiful, sea-bound tower. She wouldn't play your games. And finally she outwitted you. For the son you made me for – the son she refused to recognise – had no joy, in the end, from me. And Lleu couldn't take another wife once I was gone; his mother's curse still holds true.

So there you are, Gwydion; there you are. Challenged not just by one woman, but two. And defeated by both of them – a sister and a daughter. Tell me, now – how does that feel?

I see you twitch, Gwydion; I see your eyelids flicker. I see you flinch in your sleep. What are you dreaming of, old man? Are you dreaming of the way things used to be? Or are you beginning now to dream of me?

It didn't begin well for Lleu; I can see that now. I used to feel sorry for him, you know. You always blamed Arianrhod for his fate, but I've learned the truth: all of it started with you.

It never ends well when you take your own sister unwilling to your bed. Not nearly as clever as you think you are, old man. Cock-ups all round, if you'll forgive the pun. How could you imagine she would ever love those boys? Poor little Dylan, drowned at sea; Lleu, impotent in every way. What a fine young husband you made me for, Gwydion. What a fine rich life you offered me.

She told me all about it; we've become quite good friends. I fly to Arianrhod in her night tower; I sleep there safe sometimes, during the day. She has made me a roost in the rafters of her silver-wheeled roof. I doze there, and dream; I plan my revenge. We know about revenge, your sister and I; we know all about you too. We see you, Gwydion; we know exactly who you are.

You had a bit of a taste for rape, didn't you? You and your fine young brother. Yes, Arianrhod told me about that too; she told me how it all began. Gilfaethwy didn't have your powers, but still you made sure he had the woman he wanted. The virgin foot-holder of Math himself. Sweet little Goewin deserved better – but at least Math had the decency to marry her, after you forced her maidens from the room and looked on calmly while your brother tore her open. In Math's own bed, Gwydion! Did you have no honour at all? Still, you had your punishment for that, after Math turned you both into animals and made you mate with each other. Funnier man than he seemed, old Math. One year as deer, another as pigs, and a third as wolves in the wildwood. Did you and Gilfaethwy like that, Gwydion? Did it make you feel good? Did it make you feel like a man?

But who knows what you were thinking, to suggest that Arianrhod replace Goewin. Arianrhod, a virgin? Were you out of your mind? Had you fooled yourself into forgetting your crimes? So very surprised you were, when out the babies popped. 'I had no idea,' you said to the astonished king. 'Can't think what could possibly have happened.' Well, there was no hope for Dylan from the start; he fell into the sea and drowned. But weren't you just the generous little benefactor, taking on poor forsaken Lleu. And such a fine foster-father, wanting only the best for his ward.

Lleu didn't know he was your son, you know; he still doesn't know to this day. You'd never have told a story which might have cast you in a poor light, of course – but the truth was never your forte, either. And Arianrhod was just too ashamed. I've heard the stories you told about her; I've heard the lies you spread. Tell your lies, Gwydion, tell your lies. You can't hide from the truth. I'm the truth, little man – and you're going to find out that you can't hide from me. *Hard-hearted*, you called her, and *callous*. *Wicked*, you said to her face. What did you expect of her, really, I wonder? Did you honestly think she'd follow your lead? Preserve a line with its origins in incest? Play the proud mother, act the doting grandmother, while you stood in the shadows, plotting and plundering down all the years to come? She wanted no issue from a child born of such sin. She wanted no issue from a son of yours. Your line will die with Lleu, Gwydion; that's the one thing which gives her pleasure today. So why then wouldn't she curse him? She did him no harm, but she wouldn't have him named. She wouldn't have him armed, and she wouldn't have him married. No wife for Lleu, she declared; no chance of another child born from that disgrace. Stopped you in your tracks there, old man; your sister is no mean enchanter. So: Lleu. The accursed one. Never to marry a woman of flesh.

But you weren't a man to give up, were you? Oh no, never you. Couldn't be outfoxed by a woman; always had to have the last laugh. And ah, but weren't you the fine sorcerer, in your long campaign of deceit. You conned her into giving him a name, then you tricked her into giving him arms.

And finally, in spite of her, you conjured him up a wife.

Do you see them, Gwydion? – I do. Every time I close my eyes. Two men standing in a clearing in a wood, conjuring a woman from flowers.

She shakes the pollen from her hair, and smiles.

You think you created me, but I had life before you changed me. Did you ever think of that? Yours was never the power to create life – only the spells to reshape it. Do you know what I was before you tore me up? Before you forced me into this cold, hard world of men? I had roots, Gwydion, and they went deep. Deep and strong in the fecund warmth of the earth. Roots reaching down, roots reaching out, roots entwined with the roots of others. I rose each year with my leafy banquet, and I flowered gladly for butterflies and bees. I was made to open, and I opened myself willingly to your Lleu. Until he taught me to close.

You ripped me out of my life and refashioned me for your

own ends. Did it make you feel like a god, Gwydion? And do you feel like a god now?

You grow old, little man – you grow old.

You *dared* to judge me? – you made me. From meadowsweet, broom and oak. What did you think a flower was? – all soft petal and rich scent? Did you only think of the blossoming times, face turned to the sun and head bobbing prettily in the breeze? *Blodeuwedd*, you called me: Flower-Face. Doesn't it sound pretty, now; doesn't it sound nice?

But I'll tell you what a flower is, Gwydion; I'll show you the truth at the heart of my power. A flower can poison a man or a beast; a flower can swallow a fly whole. I'll tell you the secrets of the flowers you made me from; you tell me, in turn, if you're surprised at what I became.

My heart is made from oak, the sacred tree: the gateway to other worlds. Ancient, enduring, long-lived oak. It doesn't know how to give up. It's a hard old tree, the oak; so easy to resist the pests who try to bring it down. You made me from the tree of kings; from it, you fashioned the heart of a queen. Do you see now the strength of my heart, old man? Do you begin to understand your error?

And then there was broom: tenacious, deep-rooted broom. Do you know what they say about broom, Gwydion? – it's unlucky to bring it indoors. Unlucky for Lleu, for sure. Maybe he never heard the old sayings; maybe he never thought they applied to me.

Sweep the house with blossomed broom in May
Sweep the head of the household away.

Do you honestly think you were wise now, to make me from blossoms of broom?

Ah, but pretty meadowsweet, everyone's favourite; how could there be a catch in that? The delicate lace of its petals, a scent that's sweeter than honey – no headache, it's said, can stand in the face of it. But the truth of meadowsweet runs deeper than that; did you never think to find out? Is the lore of flowers too low for a great enchanter like you? Flowers, I suppose, are mostly the province of women. You should have thought of that, before you usurped a woman's power. You should have thought of that, when you chose to make me from flowers. Because it's a perilous plant, meadowsweet: too much of it can lull a man to fatal sleep. And are you sleeping deeply still, now, Gwydion? In the arms of the richly scented night, where its pretty white petals are scattered through sky like stars?

Oh, don't moan in your sleep, little man – I'm not going to kill you. That would spoil all my fun.

Oak, broom and meadowsweet: three fine, fit flowers. Whatever did you think you could make from such flowers? What on earth did you think I would be? At the end of it all, you told Math I'd turned wild. I guess you'd forgotten you made me from wild. I'm a force of nature, by design.

So do you fear me yet, Gwydion?

You will.

His name means light, but his was a cold light, and hard. Lleu wasn't a cruel man, but there was little warmth in him, all the same. A fair ruler, I'll give him that – but it's easy to be fair when passion's the thing that you lack. It's easy to be fair when you don't really give a damn. And he might have been named for his 'skilful hand', but his fingers could never arouse me.

Me, though, I was made to open; I was made to bloom. I was made to give, Gwydion – but what did any of you ever give to me? Instead of giving, you gave me away. You made me from flowers to give to a man as his slave. You gave me to a man who could not love me; you gave me to a man who would not even look me in the eye. I was never a real woman to Lleu; I was merely a doll, made for his pleasure.

Well, that man had no pleasure from me.

You dared to judge me? – I fell for a man whose smile was as warm as the sun. My body bent to him, my face turned up to him, and I opened like the flowers from which I was made. Oh, it was a lucky chance indeed that took Lleu away from home that day. The day that the lord of neighbouring Penllyn found himself and his hunters in need of shelter. And I loved that lord from the moment I saw him. Gronw didn't care whether I was made of flowers or flesh; he didn't disdain me, like Lleu. He came to my bed and set me aflame; he drank of my nectar like a bee.

You judged me, but what choice did you give me? In my world, you make no sense. Nature has no truck with owning, but owning is the root of all your human law. It is a sin, you say, to kill a husband – but is it not then a sin to kill a wife? For I was wilting, Gwydion; I was dying. Then Gronw rained down in me and gave me life again. You left me no choice.

In order that I might take back my life, Lleu Llaw Gyffes had to die.

Do you think I hesitated for a moment? Did you ever hesitate for me?

The sins of the fathers will surely be visited on the sons.

He was a clever one, Gronw; he was crafty as a fox. Faithless at the end, but then what man is not? It was Gronw who decided how we'd do it – how the shape of our fate would be drawn. 'There is only one thing to do,' he told me, and I can tell you that he was right. The stories said Lleu was invincible – but in all the best stories, there's always a way. In all the best heroes, there's always a flaw. So he planned and he plotted; he gave me the task of discovering how my husband might die.

Oh, look at him, Gwydion; look at Lleu there, as he struts on the stage I've made for your dreams. Have you ever seen a more ridiculous sight? What a way for a great hero to die! It makes me laugh to think of it still. See the wooden bathtub that we made for him by the river, at his own behest. Roofed with an arch made from straw. Look at him – Lleu, the distinguished lord – struggling to keep his balance. One foot planted on the edge of the tub, and the other on the back of a feisty billy goat, quivering and ripe for the rut. A stinking goat indeed! See how Lleu grimaces even as he waves, cheerfully showing me the only way to achieve a deadly blow. That was Lleu: sharp as a knife, eh? He'd even washed himself in the bath we'd warmed for him. Pity to waste the water, you know. But wasn't it kind of him, to show us exactly how the impossible deed of killing him could actually be achieved?

You wouldn't think he'd be quite so stupid, would you? You wouldn't imagine him so naive. But the scent of meadowsweet is seductive; it can quite go to a man's head.

Well, you know how the rest of the story goes. Gronw, the great hunter, cast the spear at his motionless prey . . . and Gronw, the great hunter, missed. The spear didn't kill Lleu as it should have; it lodged itself in his side. And off he flew, off and away. Off and away in the form of an eagle, off and away to the woods.

There's an irony in every story, isn't there? Have you thought of the irony in this? That Lleu the eagle found his refuge . . . at the top of a giant oak! Oh, come now, Gwydion – not even the glimmer of a smile? – but then humour was never one of your virtues; silly of me to forget. Well, no matter; you found him there in the end. With the help of your old friend, the pig. There he was, poor deceived Lleu, rotting away in the tree-top. His maggot-ridden flesh dripping to the ground and fertilising the roots of the mighty oak. Tasty meat for a common pig, to feast on the flesh of a lord. And there you were again, right on schedule, ready again to save your son. He was the only one you ever rescued; the only one you never betrayed. Did you love your son then, Gwydion, after all? Did you love somebody, after all?

You dared to judge me – but what made you think I should live by your perverted laws? Laws which preserve the honour of men at the expense of all other things?

You judged me anyway, Gwydion; then you came for me,

and I ran. Oh, I admit it freely: I ran. My newly restored husband had killed Gronw, so what refuge remained for me? I feared you then, and I had good reason. I fled with my maidens; you forced us down to the river, and you laughed as all my lovely ones drowned. There's no pity for women in your world of men. No pity for them, or for me.

I see it, Gwydion; I see it still. I see our showdown, still. Do you? I see you there, forbidding father – the father I disobeyed. You didn't seem to like it then, when I named you father. 'No child of mine,' you snarled. But we were both your children, Lleu and I, each in our different way. One child you made from incest and the other you formed from flowers. You married them to each other, just the same.

Yes, I see you, I hear you, I smell you there still, so very sure of your power. King on one side and God on the other – God on your side, for sure. Your God seems always to side with men; what hope for a maiden of flowers?

You gave me no choice: you unmade me again. What choice, then, should I give you?

An owl. And you thought you were cursing me! You turned me into an *owl*. Silent hunter, merciless murderer, powerful old woman of the night. Such a gift you gave me, Gwydion; your curse rather backfired, don't you think? You gave this flower-maid wings, and more: you gave her the gift of the dark.

'You'll never dare show yourself in daylight,' you said – but did you never grasp the power of night? 'For fear of other birds who'll despise you,' you said – but no bird can strike fear in the heart of an owl. You imagined you were condemning me; instead, you freed me – a word I would never have otherwise known. No freedom, you see, for a slave. No mind of her own. Just an empty little head, filled with flowers.

Do you see me, Gwydion; do you see me now, at the moment you utter your curse? Do you see the sparks catch fire in my eyes, the clenched fists that clutch so tight at life? 'Disobey the men,' I whisper to the trees as the spell takes me over and I start to turn. 'Grow feathers,' I say, as body convulses, as bone crunches and sinew stretches. 'Spread wings. Screech. Flap. Fly.'

Defy the fathers, fly from the fathers; fly fast and fierce and far.

You're awake now, Gwydion, and I'm watching you shiver; I'm watching you rub your eyes. I'm watching the birth of your sleeplessness; you're going to become quite the night owl. Because you see me now, don't you, at last? You see me properly for the first time. You see the imprint of my wings on your frost-covered windows, as my white face rises up out of the dark. Do you know me, old man? Do you know my long gaze? I'm the hunter, the haunter, the watcher in the dark. Look at you, there, my fine creator. Cowering in your bed against the terrors of the night. How does it feel now, to be a god?

Don't leave this window open when you take to your bed tomorrow, Gwydion. Shut your window tight against the night. I'm an owl, a silent predator; you won't even see me coming.

Sweet dreams, then, Daddy. Sweet dreams.

NO COUNTRY FOR OLD WOMEN

Even stones have a love, a love that seeks the ground.

Meister Eckhart

'When I was a young lass,' the old woman mutters to herself, as she closes the red-painted front door of the cottage behind her, 'the ocean was a forest, full of trees.' She has long white hair, is small and stooped, and mutters to herself quite a bit, these days. You can call her the Cailleach, though she's had many other names over the centuries. Beira, Buí, Garravogue, Cally Berry, the Old Woman of Beare. And when she was a young lass, the ocean *was* a forest, full of trees.

She's out and about in this newly hatched month of May before the sun has risen, though the fullness of the moon offers her just enough light to see by. Even though her eyes are failing now. Failing, but the blue of them is as bright as ever. Blue as lapis lazuli; blue as a Connemara lake on a clear, crisp winter's day. Some things don't change, even when you're old. Though mostly, things do. Yes, there's just enough light to pick her way down to the lake before the sun begins to rise, and the dog who lives with the old shepherd on its northern shore sets up his usual barking. If the dog barks before she gets herself into the lake, it'll all be over. And she's running a little bit late, this morning. Her old joints aren't what they were, and last night before she went to bed, she forgot to bank up the old Stanley range with turf. So the fire had gone out and she'd been slower than usual to dress herself, all a-shiver in the still-chilly spring air.

It's hard, being old – but it's not as if that's anything new to her. Being old is something she's done often enough before. Every hundred years, to be precise. Down all the long aeons of her existence. She counts her age not by the turnings of the sun, but by the geological upheavals of this ever-changing planet. And every hundred years, just at the point where she feels so desperately decrepit that she can't possibly go on, the time comes around once more. To grow young again – to renew herself, transform herself. The time to go down and bathe herself in the lake. On Bealtaine morn, before the sun rises and before the first dog barks. Otherwise, she's dead.

It's hard enough being old, but dead? She's been alive so long that she can't imagine what that might be. Has no idea what it might entail, for a being such as her. She's not entirely sure that she can die at all, if the truth be told. Though increasingly she's been wondering. If it wouldn't be a relief, after all. These are difficult days. She's seen difficult days before, but somehow these feel different. They feel like the end days – though she's seen those before, too. She remembers the Great Flood as if it were yesterday. Not that the Flood had presented any problem for her. In those times, she'd walked the land as a giantess, and the ocean's flood-waters had simply come up to her waist – rather than, as usual, to her knees. But she's diminished now, as well as old. She's not sure she'd have the stamina to wait out another Flood. Her strength has faded, along with human belief. And belief in her has been dwindling for centuries; so few now even remember her name. Even fewer can pronounce it. So she wonders whether it isn't time to abandon her long vigil – for, anyway, what could possibly be done now to hold back the tide of men? These days, if truth be told, she feels powerless. Powerless to prevent their growing atrocities, to insist that they restrain themselves and hold to the balance, as once she could.

She treads carefully down the rocky track to the valley below: if she were to fall now and fracture a leg, she'd be done for. She loves this valley; it's a garden of great stones. Stones whose unfoldings and flowerings have taken place not in the space of a solar year, but over the long geological ages of the Earth. Rocks uprooted and rerooted by the passage of time, and the movement of great glaciers. And she is this Earth's gardener. A rock gardener, a stone teller, a stone tender. She knows these rocks, every one of them; they're her people, her children, her tribe. Each one has its own unique character; each one its own particular way of expressing the essence of stone. She has known them through all their long metamorphoses, seen them born from pressure, torn from fire. Yes, she has stood firm as the ground shifted around her through all the long ages. As plates swivelled and continents drifted; as volcanoes erupted and meteors fell from the sky. She's seen glaciations and desertifications, seen forests wither and die, and peat form from their ancient bones. She's strode along the glacier paths, sat on the highest summits and watched the burning deaths of a million stars.

But she fears that the stones' voices are fading these days, dissolving into ever-longer stretches of sleep. For who is there to keep them awake, now? To sit with them, and talk to them; to rest in their lichen-covered arms like a lover? Who will listen any more to their long, slow songs; who understands the language of stones? Not these people, for sure. They don't even know that the stones are alive. And the stones' sleep is uneasy now; their dreams are fractured and torn. It's all she can do to wake them up, sometimes; it's all too much for her to do alone. Yes, it's powerlessness that squats in the heart of her now. She's powerless to shore up the bedrock of the land, to strengthen it against the ever-increasing violations.

This land, she sighs; this beautiful, singing land. This carefully drawn map, this sculpted reflection of her own strong body. She does not remember a mother of her own, but she has been mother to mountains, dreaming them into being through the first fiery eras of the Earth. She can feel their growing anger now, their grim desperation, as dark as the looming storm-clouds they gather around themselves each day. She senses them shifting at their roots; she feels their longing to erupt. There is little she could do, now, to stop them.

She turns the corner, and there it is: all a-glimmer through the trees, its mirror-like surface reflecting the fading light of the stars. Even the stars aren't as bright as they used to be – though here, in these wild and little-populated hills of Connemara, they're as bright as they're ever going to get. She pauses for a moment to catch her breath; she nods to the Great She-Bear and slips a wink to the Pleiades. Sweet little sisters; she remembers the night sky without them. She was walking this Earth long before they were even born.

To the human eye it wouldn't look like a particularly splendid lake, and, besides, lakes are ten a penny in this wild, western waterworld. But it's a long lake, and deep. Deep and bright, and its waters so clear that it was teeming with sleek-backed serpents, back in the day. Yes, back in the day. When she was a force to be reckoned with, when she danced across mountain-tops and leapt across continents. When a pack of wild wolves ran alongside her, and rich was the milk that flowed from her fine herd of deer.

But she's old now, and much reduced. Moss and lichen gather in the folds of her apron. A hundred years have passed since last she came down to this lake and made herself young and beautiful again. Young and beautiful and strong. And now the time has come around once more. To lower herself carefully into the smooth, calm waters; to transform herself, and take up the mantle of life again.

Ah, but she's tired, now. She's exhausted at the thought of doing it all over. Exhausted by the responsibility, by the long slow ages without rest. She is old, and tired, and forgetful. She chuckles for a moment as she stumbles down the path; she's had some fine moments of forgetfulness in her old-woman years, before. The best of them was that time when she left the lid off the well – the one where she'd water her cattle when she took them with her to graze awhile in the green hills of Beara. When she went back to tend to the stones in that land she'd once inhabited. Just one of the many places she'd lived in over the years. A fistful of her centuries she'd spent out east, and a scattering of them up north. A handful across the sea in Scotland; a precious few on Manannan's Isle. She has left her traces in those places. Her giant footprints etched forever in the rock for those with eyes to see them; carvings of her own silhouette in hills and sharp-faced sea cliffs.

But anyway: the well. A grand old well it was, too – right there on the hillside which looked out to the island. Oileán Baoi: the Island of Buí. That was the name she took then; that was her name, in that place. There was a great stone lid on that free-flowing well, and as soon as she arrived there in the mornings she would lift off that lid and let the cows at the water for a drink. And she knew all right that if she didn't place the great stone lid back onto the well before the sun went down, the waters would flow out of it and it would flood the whole world. It would pour out of the well and cover the whole world with a flood. Well, she was there one time, when she was growing old and weak, just like she is now. When it was getting close to the time to renew herself. And so, when she sat down next to the well, she found herself tired, and began to nod off. But something shook her awake with a start. The water was roaring out of the well and the sun was just coming down. She sprang up and she shoved the great stone lid back down onto that well, and she saved the whole world from being flooded a second time. But a new lake was born in the fair county of Cork at that time. A lake that hadn't been there before the well had overflowed.

She chuckles at the memory, and a sudden swift wind tumbles down the valley and whips around her knees as if to laugh along with her. She looks behind her, back up at the mountains, and sighs. Yes, she was mother to these mountains; she made them, as she's made so many more. Carried the great rocks in her apron, let them fall, and land then where they chose. But the mountains are restless now, and the old god hasn't been heard of for a while. They think he's dead, the folk around here; the only stories they tell of him are the ones which say that St Patrick killed him. Threw him into his own dark mountain lake, along with his beautiful white bull. Drowned him, they say: the dark old crooked one gone for good. It's all stuff and nonsense, of course; that silly little man couldn't have killed a fly. A hopeless creature he was, Patrick; but a meddler and mischief-maker all the same. She can't imagine why they placed him on such a pedestal.

Yes, she met Patrick, of course, back in the day. Met them all. All of them came looking for her, sooner or later. And all of them challenged her – every last one. She's heard all the stories about how they killed the old Cailleach. St Caitarin, down in Beara, who chased her across the rocks, they say, after she snatched away his Bible while he was dozing in the sun. There's even a carved stone there, put up by the *authorities*. Says that he killed her for her audacity. And just beyond the inscription, a fiercely weathered rock which they say is the stone into which he turned her. A fine man he would have been to have had a chance at it! Well, it was St Brendan who killed her down in Dingle, they say, and it was Patrick who killed her here in Connaught. She cackles a little to herself; the rumours of her death have been greatly exaggerated, over the years. But where are those funny little men now? Where have they been all this time, while she's been tending the mountains and rocks of Gaeldom? She doesn't believe she's met a single saint for a millennium or more. Time was, they were ten a penny. Now, they've been driven to extinction – along with everything else.

The old woman shakes her head; they tried so hard to stamp out her memory, those black-frocked Christian men. Like that funny little man they sent, one time: that old priest she made count the ox-bones in her attic. Thought himself a clever one; pretended not to know who she was. Looked her up and down with his hard, black eyes and decided she was far too old to be dangerous. And then he asked her just how old she was, precisely. For every bone you find up there in that attic, she'd said to him, you can add a year of my life. Well, he'd counted the ox-bones for a day and a night and still he couldn't make a dent in them. His hands were shaking as he pulled at the door handle and left.

Now the only bones she minds are her own. Brittle and fragile, like the rest of her. Like the sharp contours of her face, skin stretched tight over cheekbones sharp as a mountain ridge; like her knobbly kneecaps and scraggly, thin arms.

Her arms have held kings.

There are no more kings.

Yes, she's had her sadnesses, that old Cailleach, and they're all flowing back to her now. The ebb tide of memory turning to flood. Sadnesses rushing over her as they always do, when it's coming to the time to make herself over again. Like those long, cold centuries on the lower cliffs, staring out to the desolate sea. Waiting for the return of that faithless old bodach

– her so-called husband, Manannán mac Lir. Some husband he was; he ran off with some pale-haired fairy woman, in the end. She waited, but he never came back. There was a time when she thought she might not survive that particular heartbreak. She'd had so many, over the long relentless millennia. So many, and they accrue. She'd had so many kings; she was the mother of tribes. But there had been something about Manannán which pierced right to the heart of her. When she met him first, she had been young and beautiful. But he could not love her when he saw her grow old.

She stops for a second to wipe a tear from her fossilised face; an early blackbird comes to perch on her head. Gently, she brushes it away. Almost there, now; almost there. Just this one small wood to cross. The wide old oak forests are gone now, the great strong heart-trees cut long ago for the making of English ships. This thin, scrubby little wood is all that's left. But it's lovely enough, in its way. There's birch, the slender silver lady of the woods; there's fairy hawthorn and witch-willow. There are still some ash trees here; the die-back hasn't reached them yet. It's a lovely little copse, so, but her heart yearns for the vast oak forests. Destroyed, like so much else. Destroyed, for greed or sport.

The leaves of the strong ash trees are only just beginning to unfurl, just as she herself is coming to a new unfurling. Round it all goes; round, and around. Nothing ever really dies; she knows that better than most. And yet it can still be gone from you. She's faced so many losses; so many things loved and passed. Humans and their so-called gods; animals and plants and trees. She's seen the disembowelling of mountains, and the concrete dams which stem the flow of the Earth's lifeblood through its ancient veins. Her old knees have buckled at the tremors which surge through the Earth from their fracking fields and their tar sands. She's watched and wept as cement has spread like cancer over living land. These memories aren't good for her – but ebb tide has turned, nevertheless, to flood. And even she cannot hold back the tide. You have to harden yourself against the memories, in the end. If you don't harden yourself, you will go mad. And gardener of stones she might be, but she herself is nevertheless no stone. She is the Cailleach, the oldest of the old, and she has seen too much. Sometimes, she thinks it would be better to go mad.

She grits her ground-down teeth and shakes her tired head; finally, she glimpses the farthest edge of the still-gloomy wood. Just a few more minutes, and she'll be home safe. After the wood, only that gently sloping sweep of grass to cross, and then she'll come to her launching spot: the long, flat rock which leans down gently into the water like a slipway, tailor-made for an old woman's fumbling descent into the lake. The water will be cold, but clear; she will lower herself in and say the words. And a ray of the Bealtaine sun will rear up over the hills like a blessing as she rises up out of the water, renewed.

She is old, and she has done this more times than she can remember; it doesn't always go according to plan. The time the shepherd forgot to lock the dog up the night before, and him starting down the hill like an angel of death just as she got one foot into the lake. The time when her morning alarm failed her, and she hurtled down the track in her nightgown, feet bleeding and raw by the time she reached the water's edge. No, it doesn't always go according to plan, and this Trickster morning has something more in store. She smells it before she sees it; smells the blood, as she's smelled it so often before. Smells it, and then she sees it: a flash of fire-coloured fur at the farthest edge of the wood.

She closes her eyes, and feels her lips begin to move; the instinct is ancient, but futile. For who can the gods possibly pray to when their own courage fails them? Who might be there to hear them, when they themselves grow old and afraid? And besides, she has no time now. She is rapidly running out of time. She opens her eyes again and straightens her bowed back as best she can; she slowly picks her way through broken branches and mossy stones. And at the base of a crumbling old willow, nestled between two gnarly roots as if cradled in an old woman's arms, she finds the fox. Dead, and its fragile, furred thigh caught tight in a gin trap.

The old woman's breath catches in her throat, and tears erupt like lava from stony old eyes as they follow the length of soft russet fur. 'Oh, fox,' she whispers. 'Beautiful, brave fox.' But the fox cannot hear her; the fox will never hear again. Not the nasal squeak of a ripe young grouse as the night wind ruffles its feathers; not the harsh screech of a willing vixen calling from the depths of the wood. He had been an old fox, but a handsome one. He would have taken a vixen or two in his time; he would have eaten his share of grouse. But now, his delicate face is contorted still in pain; his golden eyes are tightly closed. Blood is pooled like thick, dark tar around his back paws. The Cailleach has seen so many things die, and grieved for them all, in her way. Buried the bodies of dead dogs, made land art from the bones of dead sheep. She has witnessed and mourned the passing of many beauties, great and small. But here and now a fox is dead – and who can ever know what will succeed in breaking us, after all? What will break us, at the end, after standing strong and steadfast for so many years. She sinks to the grass by the tree and strokes his dead body; her shaking hand hovers over his mangled leg. There is too much blood; the smell of it turns her shrivelled old stomach.

She has no time to pause here; she is running out of time. But time seems nothing to her now; she cannot find the heart to go. She cannot bear to leave the fox's body here, cold in the wood, and alone. And she cannot bear to see another creature slaughtered in this way. Another badger butchered on the roads, another hare mown down in the fields by their fume-spewing farming machines. She is old, and tired, and sick at heart. She cannot go on in such a world. She cannot; it is enough.

She will let go now, she thinks; it's time to let it all go. This is no country for old women. For old women who have seen too much, who have cared too much and loved too much and who find themselves loving too much, still. How can it be that still she loves so much? This is no country for wild things. No country for foxes, for the fine red deer who linger still in the mountains. Her laughing wolves are long gone, and with them her fine, bold bears. Gone are the bright, fierce eagles, and the bands of wild pigs that would run beside her across the wintered hills.

Her head sags forward on aching shoulders, and she raises her hands to cover her wet face. She cannot face another hundred years of this. The last time she renewed herself, the Great War had just ended, and there was hope. Who'd have imagined they'd do it all again? Who'd have thought, in just one hundred years, they'd have caused so much carnage? What could they do in another century, with all their implacable power?

No, she will let go. There's nothing she can do here: not any more. She cannot hold back the relentless tides of men; she is powerless in the face of them. She cannot protect the wild things from them; she cannot shore up the rock. She cannot hold the balance of the world against such hate.

The Cailleach lowers herself to the ground, and gently rests her head on the fox's slender back. She will let go; she will go with the fox. She will follow his fiery spirit into the mist. She'll lie here with his body for a while; she'll wait for the old dog across the lake to bark. And then she'll be done with it. Once she was young and beautiful; now she is old, and tired. She has been tired before, and old, but she has never learned how to die. And what is old age for, if you never can use it to learn how to die? She knows everything, except how to die. She plans to learn it well.

A small sigh escapes her, and a small sigh in reply from the fox beneath. The very faintest of sighs, and the smallest twitch of his chest. Startled, the Cailleach lifts her head.

Could this old fox possibly still be alive? But even if he is, he has no chance; there is too much blood in the grass around his feet. The damage is too great; the fox's strength is gone. Well then, she will sit with him here, and let him teach her how to die. She will die with him; she will keep him company on his journey. There will be no lake for her; no lake this fine May morning. No lake for her, ever again. No new transformation, no more renewal . . .

'Renewal,' she whispers to herself – 'renewal.' She heaves herself up into a sitting position, face clouded with thought. If she were to take the fox into the lake with her, would her powers of renewal reach to him too? Is it possible she might be able to save the fox? To save just one more bright and shining creature from the claws of this gods-forsaken world? Would it be worth it, to save just one more wild thing? One more bright, fierce beauty flashing through the fields. Would she do it all again, for the life of this one fine fox? Could she do it – one more turn of this relentless, endless wheel?

The old woman briefly closes her eyes, then opens them again with a shuddering sigh. She reaches out to the trap. She has no tool to prise open the powerful jaws; has only the strength of her own stiff, ageing hands. This Cailleach has now grown old, but she is the Cailleach nevertheless. The strength of stone threads through her bones still; a rock's resolution drums in her faltering heart. She is the Cailleach, and she will not fail in the face of such atrocity. She takes one steel jaw in each hand; she musters all the strength in her arms; she begins to prise it open. Grits her teeth as the trap's teeth bite into the soft pads of her fingers, as blood trickles down her arms and pools in the sagging hollow made by the crook of her elbows. She cries out as finally the trap springs open, as her hands fall to the ground and her own blood seeps into it and mixes with the blood of the fox.

Slowly, painfully, she clambers to her feet. She braces herself for one final effort, and with a groan, she gently lifts the fox out of its bloody bed of moss and twig. She shuffles slowly out of the wood and on through the dew-covered grass, cradling his broken body in her tired arms. Arms that have held kings, and now hold a fox. Quickly now, quickly; it's late. Soon the sun will stretch its long arms over the hills to the east. Quickly – but as she lifts her eyes from the uneven ground and raises her face beseechingly to the sky, she sees that it's already too late.

The dog has reached the lake in advance of her. The dog, in advance of her. He's getting old now, like her. But he stands firm on the shore with his tail erect, with his teeth bared and his upper lip slowly curling into a growl. Was the dog going to bark? Of course the dog was going to bark. The old woman closes her eyes in defeat; tears well up again in her eyes. She lowers her head to her chest, and whispers 'I'm sorry' to the fox. The dog growls again, and sprints suddenly towards her with his mouth open, ready to shout. Then, all at once, the dog catches sight of the fox. The dead fox, snuggled tight in her arms like a baby; sees the tears and blood which streak the old woman's face. The dog tilts his head to one side – then he whines quietly and swiftly lowers his tail.

The dog closes the mouth which he had opened, ready to bark; he bows his head to that old Cailleach, and gives way.

*

The water is clear, and cold. By the time it reaches her waist she is shivering convulsively, but she will not let go of the fox. 'Let it live,' she whispers. 'Just this one. Just one more beautiful, wild thing. Let it live.' And down she goes then, down into the water. Down into the bright, clear water with the fox. The lake takes them both, laps around them, soothes them and sings to them. Seeps through her skin and into her old bones; seeps through her ribcage and into her tired old heart. Seeps into her cells and mingles with the blood in her veins. She sings the old words and everything is singing, now; everything is alive. All you have to do is remember. Long ages unfold their wings and fly away out of her; the flood tide of her memory turns to ebb. And when finally she lifts herself out of the sun-spangled water, her body is young again, and strong.

Her ears are open again; she can hear them all now. All the new voices, calling to her. The eldering woman in the fields of Offaly who makes paintings of her; the young woman on the Kerry coast who writes poems about her. Two sisters from the land across the ocean leave flowers on her chair at Loughcrew; a middle-aged woman from the country across the sea leaves a bracelet at the Hag's Rock in Beara. Her ears are open again, and everything is new. The waters of the world are awakening, and the mountains murmur love songs in the west. Maybe it's not all lost. Maybe it's not all lost, after all.

She shakes the shining droplets from her hair, for it's time to go home, now – there is work to do. She will go first to the Pass of the Birds, and she will raise up the serpent that Patrick cast into the deep, dark waters at its peak. She will bring out the old god's white bull, too. She will roar in the ear of that dark, crooked god till he wakens, and the fire in their ancient hearts will set the world alight again.

She knows about stone; she is the Cailleach. Rock-solid and as old as time. She's a stone-shifter, a rock-reaver; she's the mother of worlds. She will walk through the prison walls they have built to contain her; she'll bring them down around their knees, if she must. She will gather together the ones who long for her; she'll show them the ways in which the needed work should be done. Tending the bedrock, tending the wild things. Tending the soul of the land. More than any other living being, she knows there are never guarantees. But maybe it'll be enough.

Something stirs in the water at her feet. The Cailleach looks down, and laughs at the sodden little fox. He is young again too, and strong. His soft fur glows like fire in the first rays of the Bealtaine sun, and his amber eyes are bright with life. '*Madra rua*,' she whispers; '*madra rua beag*.' Little fox, little red dog. And as she steps out of the water with the fox trotting along beside her, the old dog's excited yapping echoes through the valley.

The hills that are gathered around it answer back.

Notes

Wolfskin

This story is based on an old Croatian folktale, 'She-Wolf', in which a wolf-woman's skin is stolen by a soldier. She is forced to marry him, and stays with him until one of her sons finds her skin and allows her finally to escape. The story is similar to the Gaelic tales of the selkie: the sealwoman whose seal-skin is stolen by a fisherman who sees her dancing in human form on a beach under the full moon – so trapping her in her human form. In the old versions of these tales, no harm comes to the husband who steals the woman's skin and later breaks his word, refusing to give it back after seven years as he had originally promised her. But I've always preferred stories which come with consequences.

The Last Man Standing

This story was inspired by the old folk tales of fairy women who would appear out of nowhere, knock on the door of a lonely man (usually a farmer) and offer themselves up as wives. As long as the human husband didn't break the fairy wife's clearly stated taboos, their fields would grow fertile and their livestock would thrive. I was inspired by the old Irish myth of Macha in Armagh, and particularly by the old Welsh tale of 'The Lady of Llyn Fan-y-Fach' in the Brecon

Beacons. The natural setting arose from the seven years I spent living on and working a croft on the shores of Loch Broom – a sea loch in the north-west of Scotland – slowly watching the salmon farm which my house faced expand, and the old ways disappear.

I wrote this story while thinking of my very dear elderly neighbour there, Ami McKenzie.

The Bogman's Wife

I don't know any specific folk tales about women who shape-shift into sea trout, or vice versa. However, this story was in part inspired by the first verses of W. B. Yeats' poem, 'The Song of Wandering Aengus':

I went out to the hazel wood,
Because a fire was in my head,
Cut and peeled a hazel wand,
And hooked a berry to a thread;
And when white moths were on the wing,
And moth-like stars were flickering out,
I dropped the berry in a stream
And caught a little silver trout.

When I had laid it on the floor
I went to blow the fire a-flame,
But something rustled on the floor,
And someone called me by my name:
It had become a glimmering girl
With apple blossoms in her hair
Who called me by my name and ran
And vanished in the brightening air . . .

More than anything, though, it was inspired by many years living in the wild and radical landscapes of the Outer Hebrides, Donegal and Connemara, and my ensuing transformation into a fervent lover of bog and moor.

Sometimes, stories arrive in your heart fully formed. This was one such story.

Foxfire

In the Scandinavian tradition, the huldra is a supernatural creature of the forest. The word derives from the Norwegian language, and means 'covered' or 'secret'. The huldra is one of several *rå* – a keeper or warden of a particular location or landform; the huldra is the *rå* of the forest. Stories about her vary, but it is often said that, seen from the front, she is a stunningly beautiful, naked female with long hair; from behind she is hollow like an old tree trunk. In Norway she may be depicted with a cow's tail, and in Sweden she may have that of a fox. In contemporary Iceland, stories still abound of the *huldrefolk*. It is said that work crews building new roads will sometimes divert the road around particular boulders which are known to be the homes of the *huldre*. In many folk tales, the huldra lures men into the forest to have sex with her, rewarding those who satisfy her, but driving mad or killing those who don't.

Meeting Baba Yaga

This story arrived cackling, poking, and refused to go away till I'd written it. She's like that, Baba Yaga. And you don't refuse a woman who lives in a house fenced with human bones and skulls. The Baba is a wonderfully ambiguous character in

Slavic folklore; she'll help you or she'll kill you – it's all down to you. She's the classic, powerful, old creator-goddess of ancient myth who later was trivialised as a wicked old witch.

The story was particularly inspired by the beautiful old Russian fairy tale of 'Vasalisa the Brave'. It came alive out of the recognition that anyone can travel into the forest looking for the old woman of the woods, but not everyone leaves her house carrying the fire they came for.

I'd like to give credit to two fine pieces of work which inspired fragments of this story: Susan Richardson's poem 'The White Doe', from her beautiful collection *skindancing* (Cinnamon Press, 2015); and the brilliant Taisia Kitaiskaia's *Ask Baba Yaga* (Andrew McMeel Publishing, 2017) – a remarkable little volume of Otherworldly 'advice columns' from the Baba, which occupies a permanent spot on my bedside table.

For the record – like Carol, I was born in Hartlepool. And, with many apologies, I've never actually been to Totnes.

This story is for Moya McGinley, Baba-in-crime, ever free with a cackle and a rousing hot drop. Yes, we'll burn together, for sure.

The Water-Horse

In the classic Scottish/Irish folk tale of the *each-uisge* (water-horse – pronounced 'yach OOsh-ger', with a soft 'ch' at the end of *each*, as in the Scottish 'loch'), a young girl who is looking after her family's cattle in a shieling (summer cottage) in the bog, comes across a handsome young man and immediately falls in love with him. They sit together, and he places his head in her lap and falls asleep. It's only then that she notices the water-weeds in his hair and realises that he has come out of the loch and is in fact a *each-uisge*. On land, these magnificent horses are able to take on the appearance of a dashing young man.

In most of the original stories, the girl carefully puts a stone under his head so that the water-horse won't know it isn't resting in her lap any more, and runs away back to the village while he's still sleeping, so escaping him. Because every young girl knows that, given a chance, the *each-uisge* will trick you into believing that he's human, and then steal you away and carry you off to the land under the water to be his wife. Or, in some stories, he'll carry you away to eat you.

My reimagining of this old story was inspired in part by Nuala Ní Dhomnaill's beautiful poem, 'Each-Uisge', from her 1999 collection *The Water Horse* (The Gallery Press). It also owes much to designer Alice Starmore's vivid description of her youthful days at the summer shielings on the east side of the Isle of Lewis, in the Outer Hebrides, which she spoke of to me when I was living there and writing my non-fiction book *If Women Rose Rooted*. I'm also grateful for a couple of articles about local folklore by Dave Roberts on the Comann Eachdraidh Uig website, www.ceuig.co.uk.

This story is for Holly Ringland, and her big old selkie heart.

Snow Queen

The long and complex story of the Snow Queen that so many of us read as children came to us from Hans Christian Andersen. In it, two children, Gerda and Kay, are the best of friends. Until one day a splinter from an enchanted mirror – which enhances what is ugly and evil in the world – lands in Kay's eye and works its way into his heart. His childlike warmth disappears, and he devotes himself to the pursuit of reason. And then, one day, he is stolen away by the Snow Queen and taken to her icy palace in the north.

Gerda sets out to find him, and consults with many people and animals on her way. When finally she makes her way to the Snow Queen's palace she finds Kay alone there, sitting on the icy lake which the Snow Queen calls her 'Mirror of Reason', and working to solve a word-puzzle which the Snow Queen has set him. It is what Andersen considers to be the purity of Gerda's heart which ultimately transforms Kay back into the boy that he once was, and they set off for home together, presumably to live happily ever after.

The Snow Queen, in the original story, is actually quite an ambiguous figure. Although (not surprisingly) she seems to lack warmth, she certainly isn't presented as evil, and actually comes across as rather lonely – and although she has stolen him away she is, after all, kind to Kay in her way. Characters based on the Snow Queen in other books and movies (from the White Witch in C. S. Lewis' *Narnia* stories, to the various TV and cinematic movies of the same name) tend nevertheless to have been presented as evil; this has always seemed wrong to me.

The Saturday Diary of the Fairy Mélusine

This story is based on the old tale of the fairy Mélusine, which appears across much of Central Europe, though it is perhaps best known in France; the most popular version of the story was recorded by Jean d'Arras between 1382 and 1394. Mélusine is cursed to become a serpent from the waist down every Saturday. The curse has been laid upon her by her mother, Pressine, a fairy woman. Pressine had been offended because Mélusine and her sisters had taken revenge upon their father for breaking his oath to Pressine when they were babies. (He had promised Pressine that he would never enter her chamber while she gave birth to, or bathed, her children.) Pressine cursed Mélusine in spite of the fact that she had left her husband for his betrayal, and had railed against him throughout her daughters' childhood.

After wandering the world for many years, Mélusine marries Raimondin of Poitou. He is forbidden by her to see her on Saturdays, which she spends alone in her serpent form, bathing. She bears him several sons: the first with one red eye and one green eye, the second son with one eye higher on his face than the other, the third with long claws and a body completely covered with hair, and another with a boar's tusk protruding from his jaw. In spite of their deformities, all of their sons grow up to be outstanding men: scholars, monks and warriors. But one of their sons – the son with the boar's tusk – subsequently goes mad and uncharacteristically attacks a nearby monastery, killing over a hundred monks; one of those murdered is his own brother. When Raimondin hears of the disaster, he sinks into deep sorrow and begins to wonder if perhaps this event might be punishment for Mélusine's secret – because, just as her father did, he has eventually broken her taboo. She discovers that he has spied on her after he calls her a monster, and flies away, dragon-like, with a mournful cry, leaving Raimondin and their children behind.

The Madness of Mis

'The Romance of Mis and Dubh Ruis' is a medieval story about Mis (pronounced 'Mish'), the daughter of Dáire Dóidgheal (sometimes called Dáire Donn), a powerful European ruler who set out to invade Ireland. He landed with a huge army in Ventry, County Kerry, and a fierce battle followed which lasted a year and a day. Dáire was eventually slain by the hero-warrior Fionn mac Cumhaill, which ended the battle. Mis came down in the aftermath to look for her father and found only his dead body on the beach. She was overwhelmed by grief and flung herself across her father's body, licking and sucking at his bloody wounds to try to heal them, just as an animal might. When this failed to restore him to life, madness overcame her, and she rose up into the air like a bird and flew away into the heart of the Sliabh Mis mountains – a range on the Dingle Peninsula.

Mis lived in the mountains for many years, and grew long trailing fur and feathers to cover her naked skin. She grew great sharp claws with which she attacked and tore to pieces any creature or person she met. They thought her so dangerous that the people of Kerry created a desert stripped of people and cattle between themselves and the mountains, just for fear of her. The king in those parts, Feidlimid mac Crimthainn, offered a reward to anyone who would capture Mis alive. Most of those who went returned wounded, or died, and so eventually no one else accepted the challenge, for fear of Mis. Until along came a gentle harper by the name of Dubh Ruis (pronounced 'Dove Rush'). Dubh Ruis enticed Mis out of hiding, made love to her and looked after her. And eventually he brought her back to civilisation, and married her. When he was murdered, she wrote an elegy for him and then remained with their children; the ending in this reimagining is my own.

I'm grateful to Harvard scholar Edyta Lehman for sharing her thoughts on Irish-language poet Biddy Jenkinson's poems about Mis, only one of which, at the time of writing, seems to have been translated into English.

I Shall Go Into a Hare

This story is based on the widespread old European folklore which tells that a witch can shapeshift into a hare, and also on folk traditions from England and Germany about the 'Easter Bunny' (who was actually a hare) and the eggs which he is said to carry. The hare and the Easter Bunny's eggs are thought to be ancient fertility symbols. Isobel Gowdie's confession in the epigraph is quoted from 'Isobel Gowdie's Second Confession', in Robert Pitcairn, *Ancient Criminal Trials of Scotland* (3 vols.), Edinburgh, 1833.

The Weight of a Human Heart

This story is based on an old Irish literary tale called 'The Wasting Sickness of Cú Chulainn'. In it, Cú Chulainn (pronounced 'Koo HUllen'), the warrior-hero of Ulster, has for some time been married to the beautiful Emer (pronounced EE-mer today, but AY-ver in Old Irish), but has proven to be constitutionally unfaithful. One day, he is with his companions by a lake when a pair of beautiful white seabirds fly over. The birds are in fact Fand, the Otherworldly wife of Manannán mac Lir (who has apparently abandoned her), and her sister Lí Ban. In order to offer them as a gift to a woman who loves him, Cú Chulainn hurls stones at the seabirds, one of which passes through Fand's wing feathers; the two birds fly away. Later, Fand and Lí Ban return in their female forms and confront him on the shore of the lake. They beat him with sticks until he falls ill and lies in his sickbed for a year, unable to rise. Cú Chulainn eventually regains his health when he agrees to travel to Fand's Otherworldly island and help her in a battle against her foes. He and Fand then become lovers.

Emer hears of this and decides she cannot tolerate this new betrayal. She travels with fifty of her women to Fand's island, with a plan to attack the couple and kill them with knives. But when Emer meets Fand and sees the strength of her love for Cú Chulainn, she decides instead to give him up. Fand, touched by Emer's generosity, and realising that Emer is in fact a wife who is worthy of him, decides instead that she will be the one to give up Cú Chulainn, and return to her own husband. And so Manannán and Fand are reunited, and he shakes his magical cloak of mists between Fand and Cú Chulainn so that they may never meet again. Cú Chulainn and Emer eventually drink a draught of forgetfulness, brewed by the druids of Ulster, to wipe the entire sequence of events from their memories and allow them to live in harmony again.

I've never been a fan of Cú Chulainn, as you might gather from the story. It gave me the greatest of pleasures to imagine an ending in which Emer frees herself from him for good.

Flower-Face

In the fourth of the *Four Branches of the Mabinogi*, a collection of Welsh medieval tales, Blodeuedd (Middle Welsh: 'flower-faced'; pronounced Blod-EYE-weth) is fashioned from flowers by Math, King of Gwynedd, and Gwydion, a devious and trouble-making enchanter. She is created as a wife for Lleu Llaw Gyffes, son of Arianrhod (Gwydion's sister), who has placed a curse on him that he should never have a human wife. Blodeuedd, however, falls in love with Gronw Pebr, the lord of Penllyn, and the two conspire to murder Lleu. Blodeuedd tricks Lleu into revealing the only, and rather bizarre, fashion in which he might possibly be killed. This requires him to be standing with one foot on the edge of a bathtub by a river, and with the other foot on the back of a billy-goat. So it happens that she arranges Lleu's death, by convincing him that she needs to be persuaded that such a circumstance really would be very unlikely indeed. Lleu allows her to construct the scenario as a test of this.

Once Lleu is in position, Gronw throws a spear at him; but although it strikes him, he is not killed: he shapeshifts into an eagle and flies away. Gwydion tracks him down with the help of a pig, and finds him sickening, rotting, perched high in an oak tree. He lures Lleu down from the tree and changes him back into his human form. He and King Math nurse Lleu back to health; Lleu then challenges Gronw, whom he kills, while Gwydion chases Blodeuedd and turns her into an owl, saying: '. . . because of the shame you have brought upon Lleu Llaw Gyffes, you will never dare show your face in daylight for fear of all the birds. And all the birds will be hostile towards you. And it shall be in their nature to strike you and molest you wherever they find you. You shall not lose your name, however, but shall always be called Blodeuedd. Blodeuedd is "owl" in today's language. And for that reason the birds hate the owl: and the owl is still called Blodeuedd.' – quoted from Sioned Davies' translation of *The Mabinogion* (Oxford University Press, 2007), page 63.

The story ends with Lleu becoming King of Gwynedd.

I couldn't allow Gwydion's injustice to stand. In some parallel universe, Blodeuedd is definitely paying him back.

I'm grateful to Donna Daigle for allowing me to borrow the phrase 'You dared to judge me?' which comes from a poem she wrote while attending one of my workshops in Wales.

No Country for Old Women

In some stories about her in Gaelic folklore, the Cailleach (the old woman who is the creator and shaper of the land; pronounced 'Kal-yach', with a soft 'ch' as in the Scottish word 'loch') has the ability to renew herself every hundred years – to transform herself into a beautiful young woman again – by bathing in a particular lake. But a tale is told in some places (on the Isle of Mull, for example) that if she hears a dog bark or a bird sing early in the morning before she arrives at the lake, she will not be able to renew herself and will die. Unfortunately, in this old tale, a neighbouring shepherd forgets to lock up his dog on the night before the Cailleach is due to renew herself; at dawn the dog barks, and so she dies.

There are many stories in Ireland and Scotland about how the Cailleach is eventually killed – often by a priest, or another Christian figure such as St Patrick. It's a common enough theme, as a consequence of Christianisation and the consequent efforts to subvert or bury native pagan traditions. But there are as many stories which show the Cailleach outwitting the priests, and in spite of them she has managed to live on in the folk tradition, and is enjoying something of a resurgence today.

Acknowledgements

Much gratitude as ever to the wonderful women at September Publishing – especially to its founder, my lovely editor Hannah MacDonald, who applied herself with her usual skill and enthusiasm to this third book with them. I'm looking forward to more. Also to Charlotte Cole, dearest and subtlest of copy-editors, and to my agent, Kirsty McLachlan, for her ongoing support.

This kind of writing – at least for me – is a profoundly solitary endeavour. But thanks are due as always to my husband David, for seeing me through the rigours of writing another book and for picking up all the pieces I dropped along the way. And for crying in all the right places. And to the fabulous four collie dogs – Nell, Fionn, Jess and Luna – for keeping me company by a winter stove while the fires of imagination burned.

I'm grateful to my mother, for never telling me that fairy tales didn't matter, and for letting me read as many of them as I liked. And to those lands of stone and sea – the Isle of Lewis in the Outer Hebrides, and Connemara here in the west of Ireland – whose stories transformed me and inspired me, and which, it seems, are never really going to let me go.

My penchant for strange fairy tales – originals, retellings or reimaginings – has been fuelled by the magical short stories of Emma Donoghue, Sara Maitland, A. S. Byatt and, of course, the inimitable Angela Carter.

An extract from

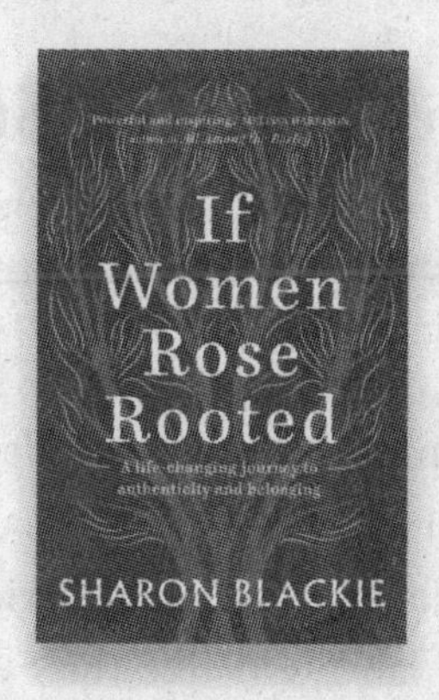

If Women Rose Rooted

A life-changing journey to authenticity and belonging

Sharon Blackie

1

Reclaiming Our Stories

It's not quite dawn in this green, fertile valley; there's just the faintest glimmer of pink in the sky to the east. The moon is waxing, gibbous, its light silvering the river which winds through the land, soft like the curves of a woman's body as she stretches out to dip her toes in the sea. A grey heron breaks the silence, shrieking from the banks as I make my way across the narrow bridge, walk slowly up the rising lane. At the crossroads, three hares are sitting quite still in the middle of the road; they scatter when they become aware of me, tails flashing white in the moonlight then vanishing into the dark.

Up I go along the stony, uneven track to the high bog, face to the Seven Sister mountains, silhouetted now against a gradually lightening sky. I wind back along a tiny path to cut home across the fields, but first I have to navigate the ford: a shallow pool in a sheltered hollow through which a deep and fast-flowing stream can be crossed. The ford froths blood-red at the edges with iron precipitates, and I creep down to it carefully, half expecting to catch a glimpse of the *bean nighe*, the Washer at the Ford – the old woman of legend who scrubs clean the bloody clothes of slain warriors. After all, this morning is Samhain,[2] the old seasonal Gaelic festival which marks the beginning of winter. And on this night, my ancestors believed, the passage between this world and the Otherworld is open.

Behind the ford is a single, clearly defined hill, a green breast rising from the soft contours of the land. It is crowned with heather, wiry and dormant now, spreading across its crest like a wide brown nipple. We call it a fairy hill, for these are the places which lead to the Otherworld – the beautiful, perilous dwelling-place of the fairy folk: the Aos Sí,[3] the people of the mounds. Once upon a time, inside a hill like this, Celtic women were transformed into the wisest creatures in the land.

In the Otherworld, wisdom is largely possessed by women, since they are the ones who hold the Cup. The Queen of the Aos Sí decided one day to bestow that gift on human women too, and so she sent out an invitation to all the women of the land, asking them to come to her great hall beneath the hill on a certain date, and at a certain time. The news was carried on the winds and the waves, by the birds and the fish; even the leaves of the trees whispered of it. Soon, women from all over the country began to set out on their journey. Some travelled alone, some came together; and when the appointed day dawned, the doors to the Otherworld opened.

The women streamed inside the hill – and gasped to find themselves in a beautiful hall which was draped with bright cloths woven from nettles and dyed with the blood of shellfish and the sap of plants. Soft animal skins covered the floors and seats, and a feast was laid out on tables of wood and stone, set on plates of pearly shell. A soft green light pervaded the vast hall. When everyone was inside and the watchers saw no more coracles on the water, no more women climbing up the slope of the hill, the doors to the outside world were closed.

Into the hall then came the Queen, bearing herself with kindly dignity, her face shining with a strange but lovely light. She carried a large golden Cup in her hand, bright with unusual marks and carvings; eight fairy women followed behind, each carrying a golden flagon of sparkling liquid which they used to continually fill the Cup. The Queen passed through the hall, offering a drink from the Cup to each of the women who was present. The Cup held the distilled wisdom of the world through all the ages past, and as each woman drank she suddenly grew wise, and understood many things she had never known before. Some were able to see much, some were able to see little – but every one of them benefitted. And then the women feasted, and the next morning they went back out into the world again, filled with the wisdom and knowledge of the Otherworld.[4]

Here in Ireland, the Otherworld is as real as any other. This is a landscape steeped in stories, and those stories stalk us still. They have seeped into the bones of this land, and the land offers them back to us; it breathes them into the wind and bleeds them out into streams and rivers. They will not be refused.

Before there was the Word, there was the land, and it was made and watched over by women. Stories from almost every culture around the world tell us that once upon a time it was so. For many native tribes throughout America, Grandmother Spider continually spins the world into being. For the Andean peoples of South America, Pachamama is the World Mother; she sustains all life on Earth. In Scotland and Ireland, the Cailleach – the Old Woman – made, shaped and protects the land and the wild things on it. In these and other Celtic nations, Danu[5] gave birth to all the other gods and was mother to the people who followed. Women: the creators of life, the bearers of the Cup of knowledge and wisdom, personifying the moral and spiritual authority of this fertile green and blue Earth.

Do you remember those days?

Me neither. Other indigenous cultures around the world may still respect and revere the feminine, but we Western women lost control of our stories a long time ago. The story which I was given to carry as a very young child, the story which both defined me and instructed me about the place I occupied in this world, accorded no such significance to women. In this story, woman was an afterthought, created from a man's body for the sole purpose of pleasing him. In this story, the first woman was the cause of all humanity's sufferings: she brought death to the world, not life. She had the audacity to talk to a serpent. Wanting the knowledge and wisdom which had been denied her by a jealous father-god, she dared to eat the fruit of a tree. Even worse, she shared the fruit of knowledge and wisdom with her man. So that angry and implacable god cast her and her male companion out of paradise, and decreed that women should be subordinate to men for ever afterwards.

The stories we tell about the creation of the Earth and the origins of humankind show us how our culture views the world, our place in it, and our relationships with the other living things which inhabit it. And the key consequence of this particular creation myth is a belief, prevalent now for centuries in the West, that women are naturally disobedient temptresses who must be kept firmly in their place. We are weak-willed, easily persuaded to think or do evil, faithless, untrustworthy, mendacious, and motivated purely by self-interest. The story of Eve in the Book of Genesis is the underpinning for countless measures which have limited the actions, rights and status of women. No matter what women might achieve in the world, the fundamental message of the sacred texts of the world's largest religious grouping, which for 2,000 years have supplied the foundational beliefs of our Western culture, is that men should not trust women, and that women should trust neither themselves nor each other.

When I was a child, this cultural story about who we are as women made me feel small, insignificant, empty. As I grew older, it made me angry. Angry, because it justifies a world in which men still have almost all the real power over the cultural narrative – the stories we tell ourselves about the world, about who and what we are, where we came from and where we're going – as well as the way we behave as a result of it. Angry, because it justifies the centuries-old violence against women which threatens even in this 'enlightened' twenty-first century to spiral out of control. That violence was endemic in my own family. My mother, as a tiny child, picked up a poker from the fireplace and held it up to her father to stop him beating my grandmother. A couple of decades later, at just about three years old, I took hold of my own father by the kneecaps and pushed him, step by astonished step, out of the room to stop him hitting my mother.

Yes, I come from a line of strong and brave women – but I grew up feeling that the world was not a safe place for us. And even though most of the men I've known during my life – the men I've loved, the men who have been my friends – find this situation just as abhorrent as I do, the story is replayed over and over again at a cultural level. In the United Kingdom, where I grew up, one woman in four experiences domestic violence at some point in her life, and one woman in four experiences sexual assault as an adult. Worldwide, the figures are higher: around one in three.[6] Political scientist Mary Kaldor has reported that in the 'new wars' waged over resources, ethnicity and faith, 80 per cent of casualties are women and children. Rape and pillage, says Kaldor, are the modus operandi.[7] Today, sexual abuse, abductions, forced slavery and forced prostitution are commonplace, even – especially – in the heart of the fine capital cities of Europe and America of which our culture is so proud. And that's not to mention the daily harassment in public places, the deeply ingrained everyday sexism that so many of us are conditioned just to take for granted.[8] This is a world in which the cultural narrative informs us that women don't matter as much as men, and so it is okay for men to do these things to them.

So many of us today accept this state of affairs as just the way the world is. We're conditioned to accept it. We get on with our lives and treat it as old news. It's okay, we tell ourselves: during the last century, feminism was born and so equality is happening and everything is getting better now. And among liberal thinkers in the UK, feminist writer and activist Beatrix Campbell suggests,[9] the optimistic belief that men and women are on a cultural journey toward equality still prevails. But Campbell argues that not only has this progress stopped, in some cases it has actually been reversed. Even though awareness of the issues which women face is high, even though lip-service is paid to women's rights, new inequalities are emerging in our culture all the time. We are living, she writes, in an era of 'neopatriarchy' in which violence has proliferated, body anxiety and self-hatred have flourished, rape is committed with impunity, sex trafficking thrives and the struggle for equal pay is effectively at an end. It's hard to disagree with Campbell that a new revolution is needed; the only question is what form it should take.

As I grew older still, I grew angry about other things, too: things that might seem on the surface to have nothing to do with the story of Eve, or the disempowerment of women – but which in fact are profoundly related. The same kinds of acts that are perpetrated against us, against our daughters and our mothers, are perpetrated against the planet: the Earth which gives us life; the Earth with which women have for so long been identified. Our patriarchal, warmongering, growth-and-domination-based culture has caused runaway climate change, the mass extinction of species, and the ongoing destruction of wild and natural landscapes in the unstoppable pursuit of progress.

At six years old, knowing nothing but somehow understanding everything, I sobbed as hazy black-and-white TV news footage showed a bird futilely flapping its wings, slowly drowning in a thick soupy layer of black crude oil which coated the surface of the sea. Another bird landed next to it, sank below the surface, re-emerged for a final few flaps, then drifted into the growing mass of dead bodies lining up along the south-west coast of England. I was watching one of the first major acute man-made environmental disasters, caused by the wreckage of the oil supertanker SS *Torrey Canyon* – 32 million gallons of crude oil dumped into the ocean, and around 15,000 sea birds killed. The sea burst into huge sheets of flames as napalm was dropped in an effort to burn off the oil. I thought the world was ending. 'It was just an unfortunate accident,' people said at the time – but how often have we done it since?

Then there was MAD: Mutually Assured Destruction. You couldn't make it up. You didn't have to; I grew up in the shadow of it, at the height of the Cold War. Russia and America, each side armed heavily in preparation for an all-out nuclear world war. Each with a nuclear 'deterrent' that was supposed to preclude an attack by the other, because such an attack would lead to immediate retaliation and the annihilation of the attacker's country as well as the attacked. The United Nations website says it all: 'Nuclear weapons are the most dangerous weapons on earth. One can destroy a whole city, potentially killing millions, and jeopardizing the natural environment and lives of future generations through its long-term catastrophic effects.'[10]

We all firmly believed it was going to happen, one day; the government even published leaflets to advise us what to do when it did. 'Protect and Survive' appeared in the UK in 1980 after a resurgence of the Cold War and, with nice little line-drawings, helpfully showed how to build your own fallout room, advising that you stock it with tinned food and a radio. It even showed how an improvised toilet could be built from a chair. You might want to do this now, was the implicit message, because when the bomb hits, it'll be too late. 'Protect and Survive' stimulated Raymond Briggs to write *When the Wind Blows*, a poignant and oddly shocking graphic novel which shows a nuclear attack on Britain by the Soviet Union from the viewpoint of a retired couple. 'Further instructions' do not come by radio, as 'Protect and Survive' blithely promised that they would; the book ends on a bleak note, as Jim and Hilda Bloggs cover themselves in paper bags, praying in their fallout shelter as death approaches and the room slowly darkens around them.

I was twenty-one when *When the Wind Blows* was published; I'm fifty-four now and in spite of all the fine work to achieve nuclear disarmament in the past couple of decades, nothing fundamental has changed. 'Although nuclear weapons have only been used twice in warfare – in the bombings of Hiroshima and Nagasaki in 1945 – about 22,000 reportedly remain in our world today,' declares the United Nations, in the enormous section of its website devoted to Weapons of Mass Destruction: not merely nuclear weapons, but chemical and biological too. So many ways not only to kill each other, but to destroy non-human life on this planet in the process. I grew up with the knowledge that there were men ready to do just that. *Dr. Strangelove* might have been funny, but it was no joke. Still, we were just women, and we were supposed to trust their judgement. 'The men know best,' said a school friend's mother after I told her I was joining the Campaign for Nuclear Disarmament because if we didn't do something about it, they were going to destroy the world. *The men know best?* I didn't know what to say.

Women might have been complicit – we had been well-trained for centuries, after all; a little bit of burning at the stake, incarceration in nunneries and lunatic asylums if we didn't do what we were told, and the constant threat of rape and violence: all of them do wonders for compliance – but the men were the ones with their fingers on the buttons. The men were the ones in charge. As a teenager I wanted that to change, but I couldn't imagine how. I couldn't even picture a world in which it might be different: a world in which women were respected and in which we got to create the cultural narrative too; a world in which men and women lived together in a balanced and sustainable way, respecting the planet which gave us life and the other creatures which share it with us. So, as so many of us do, I just knuckled down and 'got on with my life', going to university, signing up for a PhD, preparing to enter the system.

A year into my PhD, just after I'd read *When the Wind Blows*, I went with a friend to visit her aunt, an elderly retired lecturer in history. Over tea in her Hampstead flat I talked about Briggs' book, bemoaning a Western civilisation in which the men had all the power, and women had never been able to influence the way the world was. I lamented the complete lack of stories from my own country which might offer us examples of, or even just inspiration for, women who were respected and could lead. She shook her head, levered herself slowly out of an ancient, dusty armchair and sifted through her bookshelves until she found the thick paperback she was looking for. 'Read this,' she said, putting it into my hands. 'It wasn't always so. It doesn't have to be so. Women could be leaders once, in this country; there were strong women, who influenced the way things were. It was long ago, but that doesn't mean it can't happen again. You're young; read about those women, and then decide what you are going to do to change things.' The book she gave me was called *The Eagle and the Raven*, and it was a historical novel by a writer called Pauline Gedge.[11] It was in good part about Boudica: the woman who fought the Roman patriarchy in the first century AD, and almost won. I left, devoured the book in a single weekend, and then tracked down everything else I could find about her in the library. There was virtually nothing; most of the history section seemed to contain books about men.

Boudica[12] was a member of the Iceni, who occupied an area of England roughly equivalent to modern-day Norfolk. They were one of many tribes of Celtic-speaking people who lived in Britain from the Iron Age through to the coming of the Romans and the subsequent invasion of the Saxons.[13] 'In stature she was very tall, in appearance most terrifying, in the glance of her eye most fierce, and her voice was harsh,' Roman consul and historian Cassius Dio said of her. 'A great mass of the tawniest hair fell to her hips; around her neck was a large golden necklace; and she wore a tunic of divers colours over which a thick mantle was fastened with a brooch.'[14] Following the Roman invasion, Boudica's husband Prasutagus had ruled the Iceni as a nominally independent ally of Rome. When he died, his will – in which, contrary to protocol, he left his kingdom jointly to his daughters and the Roman Emperor – was ignored. His lands and property were confiscated; his nobles were taken into slavery. And, according to Tacitus, Boudica was flogged and her daughters were raped.

While the Roman governor Gaius Suetonius Paulinus was away leading a campaign against the island of Mona (modern Anglesey) – a refuge for British rebels and a stronghold of the druids – the Iceni conspired with their neighbours the Trinovantes and others to revolt. Boudica was chosen as their leader, for, as Tacitus said in the *Annals*, 'the Britons make no distinction of sex when they choose their leaders'. Boudica and her people destroyed Camulodunum (modern Colchester), Londinium and Verulamium (St Albans). Suetonius returned and regrouped his forces in the West Midlands; before the battle against him began, Boudica spoke to her troops from her chariot, with her daughters beside her. If the men wanted to live in slavery, then that was their choice, she declared: but she, a woman, was resolved to win or die.

Sadly, this time around the Romans won the battle, and it was said that Boudica poisoned herself after the defeat. More was lost, of course, than just a battle. The Romans remained, and the people were weakened. There were no more tribal queens: the Romans considered female power to be a sign of barbarism. The Anglo–Saxons came, the country converted rapidly to Christianity, and the patriarchy took firm hold. And yet, and yet . . . Boudica may have lost, but still she fought, and still she led. A woman from my culture, out of my history. I allowed myself to develop a fantasy. What if women rose again? Not in battle, but what if we could reclaim, somehow, that power and respect which women had lost? What if we could somehow dismantle this planet-destroying patriarchy, and recreate a world in which we lived in balance?

It was a lovely fantasy, but I was young, powerless and poor. I slipped back, as we all do, into the needs and strictures of my own life. I slipped quietly into the system, settled for safety and security. It was a long time before I thought again about Boudica, and the lost power of Celtic women.

The world which men have made isn't working. Something needs to change. To change the world, we women need first to change ourselves – and then we need to change the stories we tell about who we are. The stories we've been living by for the past few centuries – the stories of male superiority, of progress and growth and domination – don't serve women and they certainly don't serve the planet. Stories matter, you see. They're not just entertainment – stories matter because humans are narrative creatures. It's not simply that we like to tell stories, and to listen to them: it's that narrative is hard-wired into us. It's a function of our biology, and the way our brains have evolved over time. We make sense of the world and fashion our identities through the sharing and passing on of stories. And so the stories that we tell ourselves about the world and our place in it, and the stories that are told to us by others about the world and our place in it, shape not just our own lives, but the world around us. The cultural narrative *is* the culture.

If the foundation stories of our culture show women as weak and inferior, then however much we may rail against it, we will be treated as if we are weak and inferior. Our voices will have no traction. But if the mythology and history of our culture includes women who are wise, women who are powerful and strong, it opens up a space for women to live up to those stories: to become wise, and powerful and strong. To be taken seriously, and to have our voices heard.

While the stories of Eve, Pandora[15] and other 'fallen women' may be the stories that have been foisted upon us for the best part of 2,000 years, they aren't the only myths we have inherited, those of us who have Celtic roots. Refusing to confine itself in the whalebone corsets of national borders, the 'Celtic fringe' – made up of specific regions of the countries which stretch along the western oceanic coastline of Europe – binds together richly diverse populations with a strong thread of collective cultural identity. That thread isn't founded on tribalism or nationalism, and nor is it about genetics. These entanglements emerge from shared history, mythology and common belief systems; they arise out of a common landscape and environment which brought about a highly distinctive pan-Celtic culture that is rooted in intense feelings of belonging to place.

And so, rising high up on the heather-covered moorlands of Cornwall, Ireland, Scotland, Wales, the Isle of Man and Brittany, seeping through our bogs, flowing down our streams and into our rivers and out onto the sandy strands of the rock-strewn Atlantic seaboard, are the old Celtic myths and stories.

Our own stories, no one else's. Stories steeped in sea brine, black and crusty with peat; stories that lie buried beneath our feet, which spring directly out of our own distinctive native landscapes, and which informed the lives of our own ancestors. These are the stories we will visit in this book.

For women particularly, to have a Celtic identity or ancestry is to inherit a history, literature and mythology in which we are portrayed not only as deeply connected to the natural world, but as playing a unique and critical role in the wellbeing of the Earth and survival of its inhabitants. Celtic myths for sure have their fair share of male heroism and adventure, but the major preoccupation of their heroes is with service to and stewardship of the land. And once upon a time women were the guardians of the natural world, the heart of the land. The Celtic woman who appears in these old tales is active in a different way from their heroes and warriors: she is the one who determines who is fit to rule, she is the guardian and protector of the land, the bearer of wisdom, the root of spiritual and moral authority for the tribe. Celtic creation stories tell us that the land was shaped by a woman; Celtic history offers us examples of women who were the inspirational leaders of their tribes. These are the stories of our own heritage, the stories of the real as well as the mythical women who went before us. What if we could reclaim those stories, and become those women again?

*